Contents Page

INTRODUCTION

Since the dawn of history mankind has been waging a war against disease. The conflict has been a long and hard one – sometimes it even seemed as if people were winning. But with our ramshackle collection of needles and pills, the odds have been stacked against us. Ultimately, we have been fighting a losing battle; against an adversary that travels through the air like invisible dust; an enemy that can lie dormant for years until it is ready to strike; an opponent that can adapt and transform its physical appearance when threatened.

Aside from Biblical descriptions of plague, history records that humans enjoyed their first skirmish with disease epidemic in the 14th Century. The bubonic plague that travelled to Europe on Genoese sailing ships killed one in three of the population, inspiring fear and terror. It appeared at a time when our knowledge of disease was limited. This Black Death was seen by many as divine retribution for the sins of humans. When it returned to kill again in the 17th Century, it was assumed by Church elders that people had not yet learned their lesson. They were right.

Despite the devastation wreaked throughout the world by AIDS, there is no more deadly disease known to modern man than Ebola. Like most viruses, no-one can really be sure where it comes from. Some say that its source lies in an underground stream to the north of Africa; others say that it has been on this Earth far longer than humans. Highly contagious and completely untreatable, the microscopic virus bides its time waiting to strike when we are at our weakest. It is impossible to predict when Ebola, or one of its equally deadly cousins, will choose to make its next attack. All we can do is sit and wait; keep watching and waiting until

VIRUS OUTBREAK

BY
IAN PROBERT

KINGFISHER
An imprint of Larousse plc
Elsley House
24–30 Great Titchfield Street
London W1P 7AD

Copyright © Larousse plc 1997
Text copyright © Ian Probert 1997

First published by Larousse plc 1997

10 9 8 7 6 5 4 3 2 1

A CIP catalogue record for this book is available from the British Library

ISBN 0 7534 0123 1

"You will have to make your own minds up about how many of the 'facts' contained in this story are true. Some are based on public information, but others are the result of a fictional interpretation by the author of events, what might have been said or done. Some names have been changed, as you can see, to protect the individuals involved."

Designed and typeset by Tracey McNerney
Printed in the United Kingdom

it is time to fight.

There are those who foretell that the end of the human race will be brought about by pestilence. Certainly, with our increasingly sophisticated communications systems, there has never been a better time for a virus like Ebola to launch an attack. This is the story of what happened when it did. And the tale of a group of individuals who, for a few short days, had the destiny of the world on their shoulders. Their files serve to remind us that we are never too far away from the precipice that leads to disaster. Files marked:

CLASSIFIED

CHAPTER ONE

Farr had no way of knowing that in less than six days' time he would hold the future of humanity in his well-manicured fingers. With his stiff, freshly pressed uniform and sixty-dollar haircut, anybody could tell that he didn't belong – belong underneath the bleached white light of the doctor's waiting room and the husky breath of its air conditioner. Amongst the coughs, sneezes and subdued faces buried behind well-thumbed copies of *Newsweek* and *Mad* magazine, Farr stood out as a beacon of health and vitality: fresh, impeccably groomed; indestructible; a painting in oils of an all-American boy; a testament to youth. He had no right being here – you didn't have to be a doctor to see that.

Unlike everyone else around him, Farr remained unseated, prowling around the room shooting cursory glances at the posters and flyers pinned to the medical centre walls; occasionally pulling back his sleeve to inspect a shiny gold wristwatch. Punctuality was important to Farr; he worked in a business where time was measured in microseconds. He was man in a hurry – and one who did not feel comfortable amongst the sick.

Farr's impatient vigil lasted only a couple of minutes; it was broken when an overweight nurse lazily called out his name. Giving her crisp, starched uniform the once-over, Farr could not hide his relief as he left the waiting room and its collection of sick people waiting to be cured.

"Major Farr – or should I say Thomas," smiled Doctor Rosen as Farr entered his surgery, "how the devil are you?"

"Tom will do fine, Sir," came the deadpan response.

"Oh, let's not stand on ceremony. Call me Manny – please sit down."

Farr warily did as he was instructed and eyed the doctor

with suspicion. There was a moment of silence as the forty-two-year-old army golden boy once again came face to face with the sixty-three-year-old Jewish doctor with the pronounced Brooklyn accent. Farr's eyes were immediately drawn to the imperfections of age; the unavoidable scars of time that he found so distasteful, so unpalatable. Where not an ounce of spare flesh could be found on the younger man, there was a spillage of blubber hanging over the older man's bulging belt; Rosen's teeth were stained yellow; his breath stank of pipe tobacco; the younger man's were milky white. Farr's well-groomed, well-nourished thatch of charcoal black hair was in stark contrast to the few sweaty strands of white silk that were glued greasily across the other's pink and shiny head. But for the two men's attire, it would not have been easy to guess who was sick and who was healthy. With a grin, the doctor offered a hand towards Farr, who could not help noticing the liver spots that mottled its puckered surface.

"What's happening, Sir?" Farr finally said in a brusque, businesslike voice.

"Well, Tom, there's good news and bad news I'm afraid," Rosen slowly replied, clearing his throat as a hint of mischief gleamed in his bespectacled eyes. "We've had the results of the tests I ran on you last week…"

"And?"

"…and it is my grim pleasure to inform you that, just as I suspected, you are sickeningly healthy. There's not a thing wrong with that movie star torso of yours."

The humour was lost on Farr, who held his face rigid with seriousness. "What about the bad news?" he said nervously.

"Ah, now there's the rub…" explained Rosen, settling into his leather chair. "This is the eighth time in two months that you've been to see me. Each time there has been nothing physically wrong with you. I'm rather afraid that you've got a problem, Tom."

"A problem?" echoed the younger man, unable to conceal

his concern.

"Yes, a problem!" continued the doctor. "The bad news is that I'm going to recommend that you go see a colleague of mine, Doctor Hank Armstrong – he's a psychiatrist. Top man as it happens."

"A shrink!" exclaimed Farr in a horrified voice.

"That's right – a shrink."

Major Farr felt his body tighten. "Emmanuel, the last thing I need right now is a shrink," he said weakly.

"Oh, I must beg to differ," insisted the doctor. "There has to be a reason why you keep coming to see me and I don't think it's because you enjoy my company. By the way, it's Manny – please!"

"Emman… Manny," Farr corrected himself, "you know I don't have the time to go visiting head doctors."

"Tom, since the beginning of this year you've come to me claiming to have every exotic disease under the sun; from the common cold to scarlet fever to diphtheria to rabies to Lord-knows-what. That ain't healthy. You'll just have to make the time – and that's an order."

Farr bowed his head in resignation before speaking. "All right," he mumbled, "I'll go see the shrink, but not for a couple of weeks. I've got too much work on right now."

Doctor Rosen lowered his voice and carefully scrutinised his patient. "You mean too much monkey business," he announced enigmatically.

A puzzled frown etched itself on to Farr's clean-shaven features. "I beg your pardon, Sir?" he said softly.

"Tom, I'm no head doctor but don't you think that all this sticking needles into little ol' monkeys could have something to do with why you currently come to see me more than you do your wife?" said the doctor, suddenly growing serious. "And if I have to tell you to call me Manny once more I'm putting you on a course of strong laxatives."

"It's my job, Sir."

"It may well be your job, Tom, but we both know that

you're placing yourself in contact with some pretty spectacular diseases."

"That doesn't worry me at all."

"Tom, that may or may not be so," the doctor added cautiously, "but have you ever considered that you're not worried because your poor old subconscious is doing the worrying for you?"

"With all due respect, Doctor," said Farr rather too formally, "don't you think that sort of talk is a little naïve?"

"Possibly," acknowledged the older man, "but you have to admit there is an element of plausibility in what I say."

Farr shook his head and said nothing. His eyes scanned the room, looking for something to fix on to whilst avoiding the other man's stare.

"How is the job, Tom?" asked Rosen, lowering his voice.

"It's fine. No problem at all," replied Farr, his mood growing darker.

"Why do I get the impression that you're not being honest with me?"

"You tell me, Sir."

The doctor took a deep breath before continuing. "You ain't gonna like this, Tom, but I took the liberty of giving Judy a call."

"You rang my wife!" said Farr, his eyes widening.

"She told me about the incident with the space suit."

"She had no right doing that."

"Maybe so, maybe not. Whatever the case, I know the whole story and I can't blame you for being a little freaked."

Farr's attention strayed for a moment as he recalled the events of last January. He had been wearing a biological space suit to study the effects of Marburg, a Level 4 virus, known by those in his business as a 'Hot Agent'. Whilst performing an autopsy on a dead monkey he had accidentally sliced open one of his gloves. Luckily, the protective layers beneath the glove had not been breached, but the incident had put the fear of God into Farr. Since that day, he had not donned a space suit; he told himself that he was taking a vacation from the danger that such work entailed, but a small part of him knew that this was not the real reason.

"These things happen in my line of work, Sir," he maintained steadfastly.

"I'm sure they do, Tom," said the doctor. "But if I were in your shoes I'd have been terrified."

"People react to a crisis in different ways."

"Which is why I'm recommending that you go talk to Armstrong."

Farr watched glumly as Doctor Rosen scribbled something on a piece of paper. "This is Armstrong's address," he said, "go see him as soon as possible."

"Whatever you say," said Farr, taking the note and rising from his chair.

The clip-clop of Farr's highly polished black shoes echoed in the room as he walked towards the door.

"One more thing, Tom," called the doctor before his client could escape.

"Sir?"

"I'm sorry, but if you come and see me again you'd better have a darn good excuse or I'm going to have no choice but to make a report to your superiors."

"Okay Manny – I understand."

"I'm not a fool, Tom, I realise that you're under a great deal of pressure," said the other man sympathetically. "I wouldn't like to see you go under."

Farr nodded his too handsome head and flashed a weak smile. "Neither would I," he said, absent-mindedly. "Neither would I."

CHAPTER TWO

Earlier that afternoon, Leonard had been listening to the Stones. He'd been mouthing along to the words like he was Jagger. He'd been jumping to the rhythm. He'd been wondering how that old-timer still managed to strut his stuff. Now, though, he'd turned the music off. There were other things Leonard had to think about.

Ben Leonard always found the noises that monkeys make slightly disconcerting. At certain times their cheeps and grunts became almost human; their voices reminded him of frightened little children. On those occasions, when their cries cut deepest into his soul, he found his chosen occupation a trite distasteful. At fifty-years-of-age, Leonard cut an unlikely looking figure for a doctor of veterinary medicine. A genuine refugee from the sixties, who had even been present at Woodstock in '69, Leonard was apt to form strong attachments with any of the 16,000 or so monkeys that passed through the Reston Primate Quarantine Unit in Virginia each year.

Reston operated as a bit of a 'half-way house'; its purpose was to ensure that all monkeys were free from disease or illness before being moved on to the multitude of biological research establishments that dotted the United States. Because of the similarities between simian and human physiology, an infected monkey could easily pass on its ailments to people. Everyone who worked with the animals at Reston was aware that such an occurrence could be potentially disastrous.

With his long, grey-streaked hair, Leonard had been working at the monkey house for over ten years; he was responsible for Hall H – one of three vast, stadium-sized rooms that were each capable of holding up to 450 monkeys. His colleagues at the Unit were known to raise an eyebrow in disapproval at the blue jeans that Leonard wore and at his habit of giving pet names to the sometimes spitting, often snarling, but frequently tender animals that were destined to be used as guinea pigs for a variety of experiments. It always plucked at his conscience that he was indirectly responsible for the deaths of so many of these beautiful creatures. Leonard told himself that the cost in primate lives had to be weighed against the number of human lives that could be saved through research into diseases and other unthinkable medical conditions.

Leonard was not having a good day. A shipment of monkeys that had arrived a week earlier from the Philippines had developed a problem that was momentarily making this ageing child of the sixties forget his struggle with guilt. They were dying; something was killing them rapidly and with alarming efficiency. The doctor hadn't the faintest idea what it could be. "C'mon Cheetah," he said soothingly to the female long tailed macaque that he held in his arms. "Whatsamatter?"

Macaques were Leonard's favourite breed of monkey. Despite the creatures' dog-like snouts and sharply pointed canine teeth, the animals looked and behaved remarkably like humans. In their native Manila they were sometimes called kras, because of the distinctive 'kra! kra!' sound that they made when alarmed. It was a sound that Leonard had been hearing a lot over the past few days.

Like many of the shipment, the macaque that Leonard was cradling in his gloved arms was exhibiting the symptoms of some kind of disease. Leonard had run a variety of tests on the animals and simply could not come up with a diagnosis for their condition. One by one the animals were succumbing to a mystery illness that appeared to have no cure. In the thirty or so years that Leonard had been working with monkeys, he had never seen anything quite so strange or frightening. Spotting an animal that was coming down with the disease was not difficult; the monkey became subdued, its eyes took on a glazed appearance and its nose became runny as if it had a cold. But this was no common cold that the animals were suffering from. Sometimes, it was blood that would drip from their noses.

Leonard had already carried out several autopsies on the macaques. He most definitely did not like what he saw when he sliced the animals open. It was almost as if their internal organs had been reduced to a bloody pulp; like mashed potato mixed with ketchup. Furthermore, their spleens were grotesquely enlarged and filled with hard, congealed, black blood.

When the colony of monkeys had begun to come down with the disease, Leonard had acted swiftly. The Walkman he usually carried while working was discarded as he placed a call to the United States Army Medical Research Institute of Infectious Diseases. USAMRIID, as it was known, was located a few miles away at Fort Detrick, in Maryland; it was a military research centre that specialised in exotic diseases. Leonard had immediately been put through to simian disease expert John Jackson, who requested that some samples of the dead monkeys be sent over to the Institute. They had been delivered only yesterday, but already four more monkeys had died and another half-dozen or so were displaying symptoms of the disease.

The rows and rows of cages that lined the walls of the Reston monkey house now had the unmistakable odour of death hanging about them. Leonard was sure that the remaining inhabitants could somehow sense what was happening here. The animals' behavioural patterns had become erratic, alternating between bouts of frenzied aggression and prolonged torpor. It was as if they realised that something was upon them; that something deadly was close by.

Leonard returned the sick female to its cage and took a

look around him. He peered into the cage of the big male that was the leader of the colony of monkeys from Manila. Usually, such an action would have resulted in the animal throwing itself at the bars and screaming in fury and rage. Its leadership threatened by this strange looking ape, the macaque would have been prepared to fight the interloper to its death. There was no such desire now. Instead, the creature sat shivering in the corner of the cage, its black fur looking unkempt and ill-cared for. Its mouth remained closed and a stream of mucus flowed from its flaring nostrils.

In adjacent cages sat further victims of the mystery plague. Their bodies contorted and their hands clenched into fists, they reminded Leonard of the frozen victims of Pompeii. In their eyes he saw helplessness and fear.

"It's like a funeral in here," he muttered aloud before softly smiling at the irony of his words.

"Kra! Kra!" responded the monkey in a voice that was almost a whisper.

Chapter Three

"Lemme give you some advice, Mr Leonard," said the tough Texan drawl of virologist John Jackson over the telephone, "next time you send some samples over here make sure you put 'em in something stronger than cheeseburger wrappers!"

A day earlier USAMRIID had taken receipt of a batch of spleen and blood samples from a dead monkey that had come from the Quarantine Unit in Reston. The samples had arrived by courier, loosely wrapped in aluminium foil. "No, I'm not being a wise guy," he continued. "It's just that some of our people here get a bit touchy about blood dripping on the carpets."

Over the years that he had been at USAMRIID, Jackson had grown accustomed to such incompetence. Outside the walls of the Institute, people seemed to think that there was no such thing as an infectious disease. He knew differently. The scars on Jackson's face were bitter testimony to an almost fatal bout of smallpox that he had contracted seven years earlier whilst working in South East Asia. The pockmarks that he saw every morning in the bathroom mirror were the result of a disease which everyone had said was eradicated; a thing of the distant past. But Jackson knew about the nature of diseases – particularly viruses; they were hardy little suckers. If there was any way to get to a human host – no matter how difficult – they would invariably find it. Jackson slammed the telephone down in disgust and popped some gum into his mouth. It was time to go to work.

The straight-talking Jackson had been at USAMRIID for most of his working life. As he had risen through the ranks, he had watched the Institute grow from nothing more than a bunch of wooden huts, into one of the foremost virus research centres in the US. With his pot belly and habit of whistling through his teeth, Jackson was a familiar figure around the place; his presence demanded respect – and he very seldom failed to receive it.

When the badly sealed package had arrived at the building, it had immediately been taken to a Level 3 laboratory, where it had been kept at negative air pressure to ensure that nothing nasty could leak out into the Institute's environmental control system. It had been there all night.

Carefully donning a paper face mask, a white surgical scrub suit and rubber gloves, Jackson joined his colleague, pathologist Robert Olin, in the lab. Dressed in their peculiar attire, the two men resembled fervent members of some obscure religious sect. Olin was Jackson's closest friend at the Institute; although the two men were the exact opposites in terms of ideas and upbringing, they shared a common passion for the microscopic world of bacteriology. Often their heated debates on the subject would last well into the night; or until Jackson chose to end the argument by cracking open a bottle of whisky.

"Don't wanna put you off your lunch, John," said the bearded Olin, peeling back a corner of the aluminium package that held the monkey remains, "but take a look at what we have here."

The hard little pellet of monkey spleen nestled in the foil looking like a freshly picked chestnut. The ice that it had been packed in had melted away; a trickle of pinkish blood weaved strange patterns in the sticky liquid.

"What do you think?" asked Olin, as the other man peered at the sample.

"Dunno," replied Jackson noncommittally, "what do ya say we plant a few seeds?"

"Let's do it." Olin knew exactly what his friend was talking about. He was suggesting that they prepare a culture of the virus; let it grow so that they could get a closer look at it. It was standard procedure; a little dull, but sometimes something of reasonable interest would turn up in the wash.

Jackson looked on as Olin carefully snipped away a portion of the monkey meat before placing it inside a mortar and grinding it into a pulp with a marble pestle. With this he would make the culture which would then be placed within a flask of water in another part of the lab. There they hoped to discover the identity of the disease. Inside the flask, microscopic cells would feed from the meat and grow until they divided to form more virus cells. When the culture had become large enough, a sample would be taken away for scrutiny under a microscope. It was then that a name could be given to their deadly little pest.

The process of preparing the culture took over four hours; both men were aware it would be some time before there were any results. The case of the dead monkeys from Reston, Jackson decided, would be put on the back burner whilst he got on with the very serious business of helping to run the Institute.

John Jackson was feeling refreshed from a good night's sleep when, four days later, he returned to the neon-lit confines of the laboratory. Once more wearing his surgical mask, he could sense as soon as he entered the room that something was wrong. Jackson could not put his finger on it, but there was an air of tension about the place. Bob Olin was already waiting for his colleague; his red-tinged beard could not disguise the worried frown that was stamped on to his face. "John, there's somethin' screwy goin' on in this flask," he explained.

Walking over to where the other man stood, Jackson took a glance at the flask. "Bob, where'd this sample come from?" he asked.

"It's from that Reston monkey that came in a few days ago."

Since Jackson had last seen it, the liquid in the flask had turned slightly milky in colour. Floating inside the solution he could see tiny specks of black; they looked to Jackson like pepper. With his gloved hands, he picked up the flask and took it over to the microscope. Squinting his left eye, he put the other to the lens. "Well I'll be..." he said a moment later.

Magnified many thousands of times by the powerful lens, the contents of the flask revealed a whole new universe of shapes, colours and textures. To Jackson the scene resembled a battlefield; the minuscule pieces of pulped monkey spleen had been totally destroyed by the still unidentified virus. The cells had literally exploded like an over-ripe water melon. Whereas healthy cells would usually cling to the walls of the flask as they grew, these were floating freely in the liquid like bees in a honey pot. Whatever had done this to them was bad. Very bad.

Jackson held the flask up to the light and shook it gently. A puzzled look on his face, he carefully unscrewed its black cap and waved the flask under his nose. He was aware that a virus usually smells very bad but here Jackson was surprised to discover that there was no odour at all. "That's funny," he said, handing it to Olin, "can't smell a thing."

Olin took the flask from the other's outstretched hands and raised it to his face. "Me neither," he agreed. "Nothing at all."

"Are you sure that these samples haven't been contaminated?" asked Jackson, furrows of concern appearing on his forehead.

"Positive," replied Olin, "it was the first thing that I checked for."

"In that case," his friend advised, "let's get together a swab so's we can put this baby under the electron microscope."

As Jackson looked on, Olin carefully poured some of the liquid into a glass test tube and placed it into the centrifuge machine. A stream of cool, soothing air swept through the room as the machine swiftly spun the test tube around until a globule of greyish ooze had collected at the bottom. No bigger than a pin head, it reminded Jackson of cream cheese. The precious plug of dead cells and virus matter was placed on a wooden swab and soaked in plastic resin to preserve it.

"Fancy something to eat?" suggested Jackson, glancing at the laboratory clock and noticing that it had already gone 3.00 pm. Some six hours had been spent working on their little mystery.

"Good idea," said his colleague.

Sitting opposite each other at a table in the Institute canteen, the two men picked at their food with little enthusiasm. In his booming drawl, Jackson had a theory as to the possible identity of the mystery virus. "My money's on simian fever," he insisted. "I'd like to run some more tests, though, just to make sure."

Jackson knew that the illness, although fairly common amongst colonies of monkeys, was harmless to humans; if he was right there'd be a lot more dead monkeys before the disease had run its course but at least there was no chance of anything or anybody else coming to any harm.

Back in the laboratory, Olin placed the wooden swab under the microscope while Jackson opened a filing cabinet and removed his diamond knife. With its $4000 price tag, Jackson handled the implement with extreme care. If he were accidentally to cut himself with its blade, the knife would glide through his skin as if it wasn't there, slicing individual blood cells in half. Whilst he was unlikely to feel any pain, the blade would be ruined and Jackson would have a lot of explaining to do to the people in accounts. The glinting blade was the finest cutting device known to man; it was so sharp that it could be used to cut individual slices from a single virus cell. And this was just what Jackson intended to do.

Holding his breath as he hunched over the microscope,

Jackson painstakingly cut several slices of virus cell from the wooden swab. Resembling miniature pieces of pastrami, they fell on to a drop of water that had been placed immediately below the swab. There they settled like tiny petals from an indescribably delicate flower.

The first part of his task over, Jackson slowly picked up one of the slices using an implement made from a woman's eyelash that had been glued to a small piece of wood. Jackson often joked that this method may have been crude but, boy, was it effective. After he had delicately snared one of the slices with the hair, Jackson carefully placed it on to a small metal grid. He now had his virus sample; it was ready to go under the electron microscope.

The electron microscope stood in the centre of the laboratory. Its polished metal walls towered over the two men. As his colleague looked on, Olin positioned a small box containing the sample into the centre of the great machine. His face set with grim determination, Jackson flicked several switches on a control panel and a beam of electrons washed over the sample. "Let's see what's inside this sucker," he said.

Olin flicked off the lights and the other man sat down and peered into the microscope's viewing screen; Jackson was about to get to know the virus on the most intimate of terms. The hum of the great machine filled the room. Jackson's eyes widened as he took his first look at the newcomer. "Well, I'll be darned!" he exclaimed, before falling deathly silent.

The sample Jackson was looking at was something he had never seen before. The cells before him weren't so much dead as destroyed; annihilated; obliterated by a force of unimaginable power. Images of the flattened landscapes of Hiroshima and Nagasaki sprang to Jackson's mind. And there were worms. Lots of microscopic worms, crawling likes leeches over the decaying cells. Millions upon millions of stringy microscopic worms gathering together and multiplying even as he watched. Jackson felt the blood rush to his face. For a moment he almost felt dizzy.

"Marburg... It's Marburg," he whispered.

"You're kidding!" said Olin next to him, peering wide-eyed over the other man's shoulder.

"I wish I was," said Jackson grimly. He knew that there was only one type of virus it could be: a filovirus; a Level 4 giant of a virus; a man-killer, for which there is no known cure.

"Oh no!" said Olin, suddenly feeling the need to be sick. "I think you're right."

The two men turned to look at each other in silent horror. They had been exposed to the virus; both had held the glass flask in their hands and smelled its contents. They had inhaled a Level 4 virus! Already images of Marburg victims were swimming through both their minds. Visions of tortured men and women wearing masks of blood as their skin split apart like pastry; their glands swelling to the size of grapefruits and bursting like water-filled balloons.

Unable to speak, Jackson searched his memory; trying to recall all he had read about Marburg in the text books. How long does it take to incubate? Can it spread through the air? What are the first symptoms? He could remember no answer to these questions.

For several moments, the two men stared deep into each other's eyes; the electron microscope continued to hum as Robert Olin and John Jackson considered their predicament. Both men found themselves gasping for breath. The resolute Jackson was, however, first to regain his senses.

"Let's get some pictures," he said eventually. "Then I think we'd better give Tom Farr a call."

CHAPTER FOUR

Bathed in cool autumn light that shimmered in through the window behind him, Major Thomas Farr sat in his office at USAMRIID. He had a lot on his mind. To many at the Institute, Farr was the man who had it all: good looks; a powerful presence; a brilliant mind. Farr was essentially in charge of USAMRIID; his responsibilities included the administration and implementation of every project that his staff of civilian workers and military personnel had cause to be involved in. He answered to no-one in the establishment apart from General John Kearns, who had such trust in his dashing young protégé that he seldom had cause to visit USAMRIID.

Whilst still in his twenties, Farr had pursued his passion for the study of infectious diseases by heading a military expedition to Africa to search for the Ebola virus. He had travelled the world and stepped into some of the most dangerous environments known. Amongst his fellow virus specialists, Farr was something of a celebrity; during a research trip, the Major had once entered a building containing African Marburg sufferers and lived to tell the tale. After spending the night treating the bleeding and coughing victims as best he could, Farr had emerged from the carnage somehow free of infection. To some it was a modern day miracle; to Farr's detractors, however, it was yet further evidence of his incredible good fortune.

Even in his current position of authority, Farr drew respect from his colleagues with his 'hands-on' approach; he was someone who was prepared to muck in with everyone else. Farr thought nothing of donning a biological space suit and getting in amongst the action. He liked to get his hands dirty. That is, until recently.

For the past six months, Farr's associates had noticed a subtle change in the man they had once nicknamed 'Superman'. At first, the differences were subtle: refusing to make eye-contact at crucial meetings; nervousness; an apparent loss of interest in the job that was his life.

The change did not go unnoticed by Judy, Farr's wife of seven years, who was also employed at the Institute, as a bacteriologist. Friends often teased Farr by telling him about the perils of working alongside someone you were married to. 'If you don't get bored of her, she'll get sick of you,' they joked. Farr was becoming concerned that there might be an element of truth in their words.

Farr had just hung-up on Judy. He had been telling her she had no right to talk to his doctor without asking him first. What was she trying to do? Didn't she know he was under enough pressure as it was? He took another look at his gold wristwatch. It was already past 5 pm – most of the day gone and so much work to do. These days, he was finding it difficult to concentrate on work. In fact, he was finding it difficult to concentrate on anything. He needed a vacation, a change of scenery – perhaps another trip into the forests of Africa could be just what the doctor ordered.

Farr had been so wrapped up in his thoughts that he failed to notice when the door to his office swung furiously open and two white-coated figures stepped inside.

"Major, we've got something to show you," said the voice of John Jackson. "I'm sorry to barge in like this but what I'm carrying is just too hot."

Startled by the intrusion, Farr raised his eyes and turned towards the origin of the voice. Johnson's scarred, pockmarked face was looking directly at him. The disease specialist's face was literally wide-eyed with fear. Behind him stood an equally frightened-looking Robert Olin; his beard was dripping with sweat. Resisting the urge to pull away from the panting newcomers, the Major cleared his throat and spoke. He was careful to remain as calm as possible, he didn't want either of the men thinking that they had startled him. "Gentleman," he said slowly and deliberately, "please take a seat – both of you – then you can explain your problem."

Unable to hide their surprise at their colleague's reaction, the two men did as they were instructed, settling into easy chairs directly in front of Farr's desk.

"Tom, what do you think this is?" said Jackson, without wasting any time, pulling a coloured photograph from a sheath of pictures he was holding under his arm and handing it to his superior.

Slowly, the Major took the photograph from Jackson's outstretched hand and ran his eyes over its shiny, still damp surface. The image came fresh from the dark room; it was a blow-up taken from the electron microscope, it depicted a mass of tiny worm-like spores; a million microscopic snakes packed into an area thousands of times smaller than a pin-head. The picture could easily have come from the hand of some obscure avant garde painter. "Looks to me like you've got some crud on the lens there, John," said Farr.

"Not so," cut in Bob Olin, "examine the rest, Tom, you'll find the same story in every exposure."

A slight grimace crossed Farr's face as he slowly went through the other pictures. From time to time, he was forced to raise his head and look into the eyes of John Jackson to check that this wasn't some kind of practical joke. Jackson's scars seemed to deepen as the light outside the building slowly began to fade.

"Where are these from?" said Farr eventually.

"You ain't gonna believe this, Tom," replied Jackson. "They came from a monkey house in Reston."

The Major thought for a moment. A monkey house in Reston? That was only three miles away from Washington DC; about a two-hour drive from the Institute. "This could represent a slight problem," Farr announced with great understatement.

19

The other two regarded Farr with a mixture of curiosity and admiration. The way that the man reacted in times of crisis never ceased to amaze the workers at USAMRIID. That face; that expression; it had been a common enough sight at the Institute until, everyone silently agreed, the accident with the space suit in the Level 4 containment laboratory. The emotionless expression that was currently etched into his face had been absent at the place for far too long. "You could be right, Tom," said Jackson.

"Let's try and be absolutely clear about this," continued Farr. "These are worms I'm seeing here, right?"

Without hesitation, Jackson and Olin nodded their heads in agreement.

"In that case I guess we're talking filovirus, right?"

"'Fraid that's what we're sorta suspecting," growled Jackson. "It came from the spleen of a monkey that had come down with a mystery bug at the Reston Quarantine Unit. There's a whole bunch of others out there exhibiting similar symptoms."

Major Farr sat bolt upright in his chair and thought for several seconds before gently clearing his throat for a second time. "Let's have the story, boys," he said simply. "Tell me *who* and *what* has been in contact with this sample."

"As far as we know only four workers at the Unit have been in direct contact with the sample," said Olin.

"Not forgetting the courier that delivered it to us," added Jackson.

"Have we managed to put a name to the virus?" asked Farr.

"We're not certain," said Jackson, "But the feeling is that we may be dealing with Marburg."

"Marburg!" exclaimed Farr, momentarily losing his cool at having that word spoken out loud in his office. "That isn't so good."

Farr knew all about Marburg. He had seen it in action at

first hand. He was aware what it could do to a human subject. It would make those scars on Jackson's face look like kid's stuff. If this monkey sample was what it seemed to be, then they had to act immediately. Marburg was a Level 4 virus; a so-called 'Hot Agent'; if it was treated with anything less than the utmost respect, well, the implications didn't bear thinking about. The monkey tissue that these pictures had captured beautifully, had to be placed in quarantine – and fast. Nothing and nobody must be allowed any contact with it wearing anything less than a biological space suit.

For a moment, you could cut the atmosphere with a knife; or puncture it with a needle, mused Farr, his thoughts returning to those suits. Biological space suits – the supposedly unbreachable safety garment that not so long ago had almost cost him his life. "John, let's play this right by the book," he advised. "Before we spark ourselves a panic and find ourselves knee-deep in newspaper reporters, we'd better be sure. I'm going to make a few phone calls and see if I can't get hold of some more Reston samples. I suggest that you get down to putting whatever other samples you hold into Level 4 containment."

For the third time, Farr's companions nodded their heads.

"Let's keep cool on this for the time being," Farr continued. "We don't want to find ourselves eating humble pie if this situation turns out to be nothing but a false alarm."

Farr quietly sat back in his seat and watched as the two men left the room. He could feel a vein throbbing in his forehead. The Major gulped in a deep breath and regarded the telephone receiver with caution.

Outside Farr's office, Jackson and Olin began the short walk back up to the lab. Nothing was said but both men knew that they shared a secret: they were party to a lie which, if discovered, could seriously compromise their professional standing. They had neglected to mention the fact that they had both sniffed at the flask containing the virus sample. They had good reason not to. There was no doubt in both men's minds that Farr would have thrown a fit had they admitted their contact with the virus. They were certain he would have immediately ordered them into the 'slammer', a water-tight, air-tight Level 4 holding cell that was capable of seriously rattling its inhabitants' brains. There, they would have no choice but to stay locked inside for up to forty days, watching TV and growing more and more bored with every second. Being attended to by strange aliens in space suits; unable to see their wives and loved ones; unable to contact anyone in the outside world. The slammer was cruel to those who sampled its dubious pleasures; it had been known to drive people crazy.

In lowered voices, the two friends agreed that the most sensible course of action would be to take blood samples from each other in secret; if they tested positive for Marburg they would reveal their deceit and take the consequences. If they were infected with the virus there was nothing they could do about it, anyway. It would already be well into its incubation period. A time bomb might be ticking away softly inside them, waiting to burst free in an orgy of pain and blood. Whatever punishment the Institute meted out for their improprieties would pale into insignificance compared with what a dose of Marburg was certain to do to them. They were worried men. Very worried.

CHAPTER FIVE

John Jackson removed his clothing and pulled on a green surgical scrub suit. The coarse rubber clung to his skin as he scraped the hair away from his eyes and tucked it into a disposable surgeon's cap.

"Say, aren't you Doctor Kildare?" said the mocking voice of Robert Olin, who was standing beside his friend looking equally ridiculous.

"Very funny," replied Jackson dryly, one eye on the sealed plastic carton that held the samples of the monkey spleen which they suspected was infected with the filovirus. Their task was to place the deadly package into Level 4 containment; to lock it away like a criminal and throw away the key; to send it behind bars so that nothing and no-one could ever get near it. Unless, of course, they happened to be wearing the bright blue Chemturion space suits that Jackson and his colleague were in the process of putting on.

"Man, I hate this game!" grumbled Jackson, who was still in his bare feet and staring with distaste at the door of the room marked: 'Level 2'.

Without speaking, both men entered the room and were immediately bathed in a sheen of ultraviolet light. Olin absent-mindedly thought back to his student days and remembered the embarrassment that such light used to cause him at discos. In those days, ultraviolet strobes would cruelly expose the dandruff on his shoulders as it lay like a fall of winter snow. Now it was being used to destroy any microscopic bacteria that he and Jackson happened to be carrying; it was wiping out any unwanted baggage.

Next, the two men slowly opened the door leading to Level 3 containment. There was a gust of air as they walked into negative air pressure, designed to prevent any unwanted microscopic visitors entering or exiting the room. Now they were in the room known as the staging area. Both men knew the interior well; inside there was a desk, a sink and telephone. Beside the desk stood the 'hatbox'; the purpose of this cylindrical cardboard container was to store away any infectious waste.

Jackson's footsteps were the only sound that could be heard as he moved slowly into the room, clutching the container which held the Marburg sample. The virus specialist treated the carton with the respect that it deserved. Although a major part of his mind was primarily concerned with the notion that he might already be carrying Marburg, Jackson had no desire to complicate matters further by dropping the potential people-killer. It was a mistake that he did not want on his record.

A white shower of baby powder was sucked into the room's throbbing air vents as the two men sprinkled the sweet-smelling dust on to their hands and stretched rubber gloves over them. Next the pair tore off several strips of sticky tape from a roll that was standing on the desk. Jackson and Olin took turns in wrapping the tape around the cuffs of their scrub suits; they both knew the importance of ensuring that there was no chance of exposing themselves to bacteria through the gap between gloves and sleeves. After checking that the seal was good, the two virologists then donned socks and again helped each other to wrap tape around the area of exposed skin between trouser and sock. They both undertook this exercise with the utmost care and attention. Any mistake could cost them – and untold others – their lives.

After one final check for any breaches in the plastic tape seals, the pair walked slowly into an antechamber, where their Chemturion space suits were waiting for them. They hung from hooks, looking to Olin like futuristic scarecrows. He hoped that they were frightening enough to deter any unwanted germs from straying too close to him.

Jackson looked on as his friend carefully picked up the space suit and held it gingerly in his hand as if it were made from rice paper. Slowly, painstakingly, Olin laid the blue suit on to the floor and climbed into it, pulling the material over his body until it was under his armpits. Then he slid his arms through the sleeves and slipped his fingers into the pair of heavy-duty rubber gloves that were firmly attached to the ends of the blue sleeves. He felt their reassuring weight – they were thick and heavy because they were the last barrier between Olin's body and the deadly bacteria that floated through the air in the Level 4 containment laboratory like radioactive dust. With these, Olin would handle needles, scalpels and other sharp materials; they had to be strong and capable of protecting a worker from any unfortunate accidents.

After his colleague had followed the same procedure, Olin steadied himself to put on the final part of his high-tech uniform: the helmet.

"Here goes nothin'…" said Olin as he placed the soft plastic visor over his face. Immediately his vision became blurred as the clear plastic faceplate fogged up from his breath. Straight away, Olin reached over to the wall and pulled down the coils of a yellow hose, which he plugged into a port in the space suit. There was a gush of cool air and Olin felt clean, fresh oxygen in his mouth. This was the air supply that would keep him from having to inhale the toxic contents of Level 4. Within moments, his visor had cleared and Olin looked out to see his partner donning his own face protector.

"Let's give each other the once over," advised Jackson, his voice muffled inside the bulky suit. As always he was keen to ensure that both men's space suits were free from any minute splits or other signs of wear and tear. A virus cell had no particular preference for its method of locating a host; it was quite prepared to squeeze through the most minuscule of openings in order to propagate its species.

No word was spoken for several minutes as the two men took turns to examine every part of their space suits, including the soles of their boots. Finally, Jackson nodded his head; it was the sign that everything was as it should be. It was now safe to enter the Level 4 containment laboratory. Olin turned his head towards the solid steel door labelled: 'CAUTION BIOHAZARD'.

With Jackson still carrying his lethal cargo, Olin swung open the metal door and the two virologists entered the Level 4 airlock. The 'Grey Zone', as it was called, was the final place of sanctuary before the 'Hot Zone' – the area where Level 4 biological agents such as Marburg and Ebola were stored and worked upon. It was a place like nowhere else on Earth. Jackson and Olin instinctively closed their eyes as a shower of EnviroChem hit their space suits and ran down the plastic exteriors in rivers of hissing steam. The jets of liquid were intended to destroy any minute bacteria that might have been sturdy enough to survive the journey from Level 1 to Level 4. A similar decon shower awaited the two men on the return journey from the laboratory.

After what seemed like hours but in reality was only minutes, the shower finally began to abate; with his jaw firmly set, the damaged features of John Jackson broke into deep furrows of concentration. With a gleam in his eyes, Jackson swung open the door that led to the Level 4 laboratory; the 'Hot Zone'.

After plugging into one of the many air hoses that lined the laboratory, John Jackson laid the package containing the monkey samples on to a steel table. He looked around. The sight was familiar enough but nevertheless was still a shock to his system. He would never get used to this lab. It was like another world; indeed, for all that mattered it could have been another world. The whistle of the air flow filled Jackson's helmet and intermingled with the sound of his laboured breathing. He had heard the noise many times before but, again, would never grow accustomed to it.

Although it was difficult to hear anything else from the strange otherworld that was Level 4, Jackson could just about discern the cheeping of the dozen or so monkeys that were held in the steel cages dotted about the interior of the room. Standing beside his colleague, Robert Olin could not withhold a slight pang of guilt; the animals in the cages were doomed; they were like the yellow canaries that Victorian miners once carried underground to detect gas deposits. However, instead of gas, the monkeys were there to reveal the presence of a filovirus.

There was a dull creaking sound as Olin opened up the sample container and carefully plucked out its contents. He laid them on a porcelain specimen tray that stood in the centre of a steel table. Then, with some trepidation, Olin opened a drawer in the table and slowly – very slowly – picked up a scalpel.

"Easy boy!" said Jackson in mock humour. Both men knew that one slip of that glinting scalpel could mean death. To puncture a space suit in a Level 4 laboratory is similar to jumping out of a plane without a parachute: the end result is always messy. With careful deliberation, Olin cut away a portion of the monkey's spleen and after replacing the blade, picked the sample up in his gloved hands with a pair of tweezers.

Major Farr had told them to get more blow-ups of the Reston monkey sample. This was just what they intended to do. Before any further action could be taken, the Institute had to be completely sure that they were dealing with a filovirus. If the current emergency really was caused by nothing more than filth on the lens, then heads were likely to roll.

As Olin prepared the sample, gouging the infected meat with a marble pestle, Jackson moved over to the giant electron microscope and flicked a switch on a control panel nearby. The machine instantly hummed into life.

Holding the fresh sample in his gloved hand, Olin walked over to his partner at the electron microscope. With painstaking care he placed the sample beneath the great machine's lens. Olin was aware that the pulped monkey sample would already be spewing forth a shower of minuscule Marburg particles into the air; that was, of course, if it was really infected with the virus; something that they would find out before the afternoon was over.

Within moments, a picture had appeared in the viewing screen. Both men's jaws dropped; they had been hoping against all hope that their prognosis was wrong. The picture before them, however, depicted the familiar mass of crawling worms.

"Looks like we were right," sighed Jackson, "it's definitely a thread virus that we've got here."

Olin nodded his head in solemn agreement.

"But is it Marburg," added the other man, "or is it something else?"

"Whatever it is could already be crawling around our insides," said Olin.

"Let's hope not."

For several hours the two men repeated the process they had just undertaken; cutting more from the monkey tissue; gouging it into a pulp; viewing it under the electron microscope. Each time the outcome was the same.

Jackson pulled out a reference book that contained images from all known viruses. He compared the samples against pictures of Marburg. Something troubled him.

"Bob," he said, "come and see what you think."

Olin moved over and looked at the image that his colleague held in his outstretched hands.

"Do you see what I see?" asked Jackson.

For several moments Olin did not reply. Then his eyes opened in surprise.

"Gee… we ain't looking at Marburg!" he exclaimed.

"That's what I've been thinking."

"If it ain't Marburg then what could it be?" asked Olin.

"My thoughts entirely."

Olin took the book from Jackson and waved it in front of his visor. He scanned the picture with his eyes. He checked it over and over before catching his breath. "I guess you could say that the plot thickens," he announced coldly.

CHAPTER SIX

"If this is your way of getting back at me for speaking to Doc Rosen," said the cheerless voice of Judy Farr, "you have my faithful promise that I'll never do it again!"

Three hours earlier, Judy had received a call from her husband at the Institute. This had been supposed to be her day off; Judy had been looking forward to rustling up a little home cooking for Karen and Richard, the children that were increasingly becoming strangers in her busy life. If she didn't do something about it she would forget what her kids looked like. Her role at USAMRIID as a bacteriologist was taking up more and more of her time. Initially, she had taken the call with impatience, but the tone of her husband's voice soon left her in no doubt that something big was happening.

Ten years younger than her husband, and known for her quick-fire temper, Judy had been the envy of her female colleagues when Tom had proposed to her. He was viewed as a prime catch; a man who had already been, and *was* going places. Their courtship had been brief, perhaps even lacking in a little passion. But the girl whose Irish ancestry showed in her long black hair and brooding dark eyes loved her husband for all she was worth. Which is why she had been so concerned when Tom had had the accident with the space suit earlier this year. It had shaken something inside him. There was a cog loose somewhere in that still-athletic body of his.

In a shaky voice, Tom had explained that he needed her help. There was a delicate situation developing down at Reston Quarantine Unit; he wanted her to accompany him to the building, where some samples of dead monkey tissue would be waiting for them in the back of a nearby van. The slightly, cloak-and-dagger nature of the request had sent a flush of excitement down Judy's spine; she imagined some illicit drug haul waiting for them there; she could sense adventure. Her mood, however, dropped instantly when she climbed into the passenger seat of the black Mercedes driven by her husband and saw his ashen, blood-drained expression.

"Judy, there's a chance that we may be dealing with a filovirus," her husband said breathlessly, as the lights of the freeway leading to Reston flickered in his eyes. "It may be nothing but we have to take it seriously."

His wife fell silent; no words were needed to express her feeling of horror at what he was saying. Yet, for some inexplicable reason, a smile played on to her lips.

"This is no joke," continued Tom. "The boys in the lab have a hunch that it could be Marburg. If they're right, this situation will go right up to the Pentagon."

As they neared the Quarantine Unit, Tom Farr filled Judy in on the task that lay ahead of them: in order to keep news of a potentially hazardous situation away from the Press, it had been arranged that he would pick up the infected monkey samples in secret. He could have sent someone else but, as ever, Tom preferred the personal touch. The samples were to be collected from a vehicle parked in a side road not far from the monkey house and transferred into the back of the Mercedes.

His sense of doom deepening as he watched more and more of his animals fall down with the sickness, Ben Leonard had spent a sleepless couple of nights in Hall H of Reston Quarantine Unit. By now he was beginning to grow accustomed to the sight of macaques dropping dead at his feet; he was already becoming hardened to this grisly spectacle. When he had gotten the call from Major Farr at USAMRIID earlier this evening, Leonard's relief had been palpable. The army man's soothing, apparently nonchalant tones had been almost hypnotic. After only a few words, Leonard was beginning to think that the problem with the dead and dying monkeys was not as bad as he thought. Nothing at all, really. Of course you can have some more monkey samples, Major. What's that? Double bag them and drive to somewhere secluded? No problem, Major. No problem at all.

Leonard's feelings of false optimism soon evaporated away, the moment the big black Mercedes pulled up and a worried-looking Thomas Farr stepped out to shake his hand gingerly. Followed closely by a youngish, freckle-faced woman who was rubbing her own hands together to fight the bitter night's cold. The Major immediately got down to business.

Judy was quietly impressed at how his frightened voice of a few moments ago was now replaced by a quiet, reassuring calm.

"Mr Leonard, would you mind taking us to where you are storing the monkey tissue?" Farr soberly requested.

It was Judy who spoke next. "What kind of hippie set-up is this?" she exclaimed angrily, staring at the long-haired Leonard's blue jeans with obvious distaste.

"What do you mean?" asked a puzzled Ben Leonard, who was standing at the open rear door of the van he had driven to the liaison. Inside the van could be seen a pile of black plastic refuse bags. As Major Farr ran a flashlight over the odd bundles, he could make out the shapes of monkey limbs and heads beneath the plastic, contorted by rigor mortis into frozen statues of pain and anguish.

"Jesus, do you think this is Amateur Hour?" Judy continued her tirade. "I just hope that you've disinfected those bags!"

"I doused them down with bleach myself," said Leonard defensively.

Judy gave an angry sigh: "Don't you know that this is not the way to transport a Level 4 virus!"

"Level 4 virus," repeated Leonard, turning to face Major Farr. "You didn't say anything about a Level 4 virus when we spoke on the phone."

"Judy, if you can just let me deal with this," her husband cut in guiltily. "Mr Leonard, there's nothing to worry about at the moment. Hopefully these samples will tell us that the whole thing's nothing more than a false alarm."

"Are you sayin' there's a chance my monkeys could be infected with a filovirus?"

"We haven't got the time for a debate," said Major Farr, evading the question. "We're gonna have to get these bags in to the boot of my car. We'll talk about it tomorrow morning."

"We sure will!" said a slightly dazed looking Leonard, his fingers playing with a string of wooden beads that hung from his neck. "You bet your life we will!"

Judy Farr looked over at her husband. Why hadn't he told Leonard about the chances of contamination? He returned her accusing stare with a shrug of the shoulders and moved his head towards the ominous looking packages in the back of the van. "We're gonna have to take extreme care with these little bundles," he said, with the hint of a tremor in his voice.

Gritting his teeth, Farr leaned over and wrapped his arms around the nearest black plastic sack. He felt its weight; fifty pounds of decaying monkey flesh – the possible breeding ground for billions of microscopic Marburg cells. A soft, squigy bag of bubbling Marburg soup. Cradling the deadly package in his arms, Farr numbly walked over to the Mercedes, carefully making sure that the jagged fingers and teeth of the dead animal housed within did not puncture the delicate black plastic wrapping. "Watch out for drips of blood," he shakily advised his wife.

Twenty minutes had elapsed before the contents of the van had been transferred to his own vehicle; the worry was already showing on Farr's handsome face. The beam of light from the flashlight played on the craggy lines and wrinkles that now criss-crossed his sweat-drenched profile. When he had completed his grisly task, Farr slammed the boot of the car shut as if it contained a wild animal. He knew that Judy had good reason to be concerned. He was aware that what he had just done had broken every rule in the book. He had carried carcasses that might be infected with Marburg; he had done so without wearing rubber gloves; there was every possibility that he had inhaled infected air. Farr just had to hope his request that the animals be placed in two protective layers of plastic had been enough.

Farr looked down at the hands that had so recently carried the deadly load. "Got any bleach?" he asked Leonard.

The doctor of veterinary medicine climbed into the back of the van and fished out a plastic canister of bleach. He watched as the Major unscrewed the cap and swilled some of the colourless liquid over his bare hands. For a moment it seemed that the Major would wince in pain; but he held himself together, a trail of steam gushing from his open mouth as it met the cold Autumn air.

As the lights of Leonard's van retreated into the skyline, Farr and his wife climbed back into the Mercedes. Both were covered with an icy layer of sweat.

"Tom, I hope that you're wrong about this," Judy trembled in a whisper. "If you're not, I'm afraid this isn't going to be an easy problem."

As they moved away from Reston and hit the built-up areas of the town, with its clubs, shops and crowds of preoccupied people, Judy hugged her coat to her body.

"If this gets out there's gonna be bedlam," she said as she watched her husband, shivering with the cold.

CHAPTER SEVEN

General John D. Kearns was not a happy man as he sat in the chair behind Tom Farr's desk at USAMRIID, his chiselled features lit by the bright morning sunshine. "Let me get this straight," he said in a sandpaper voice that was tinged with a mixture of anger and fear, "you're telling me that we could have Marburg on the loose?"

Kearns had not shaved this morning, grey flecks covered his chin. He had been planning to spend today on the golf course with a few buddies. His mind had not been in work mode. When he had received the call from Major Tom Farr late last night, Kearns had initially reasoned that it had to be some kind of joke. He knew, however, that Farr was not known for his sense of humour. Farr's serious tones had told him that there was trouble afoot – big trouble.

"My gut feeling is that we might end up wishing that it was Marburg," reflected the tired tones of John Jackson, who had been up all night running tests on the monkey carcasses that Tom and Judy Farr had carried into the Institute late yesterday evening. "If I'm right the situation could get a lot worse."

"What are you talking about, man?" snapped General Kearns, peering through the crowd of military personnel and bacteriological experts that had taken temporary occupation of Farr's office.

"The tests that we've been running appear to show another agent present," Jackson continued. "It seems to be related to Marburg, but subtly different."

"John, do we have a positive ID on the agent?" urged Tom Farr from the back of the room, carefully forcing himself to hold his nerve after last night's events.

Everybody's eyes were on the pockmarked face of

Jackson. "We can't be totally sure but we think it might be Ebola Zaire, Sir."

At once, the occupants of the room gave a collective gasp; then the office fell deathly silent.

General Kearns raised a hand to his jaw and settled deep into thought. "How sure are we of this?" he said finally.

"If it ain't Ebola Zaire," replied Jackson, "it's something very similar."

At once the General came to life. Sweeping his white hair to one side and biting at his lower lip, Kearns circled the room with his eyes. "Okay men," he said in a voice that betrayed its Southern origins, "it's time to go to war! This is no drill; you are about to embark upon the most hazardous mission of your careers."

Pulling a notebook from the pocket of his medal-strewn uniform, Kearns raised a pencil to his lips and licked the end. "First things first," he announced, "what do we know of Ebola Zaire?"

This time it was Bob Olin who spoke. "Not a lot," he said, standing close to John Jackson. "We know it's a distant relative of Marburg; we know that it has a ten-day incubation period; and we know that it kills nine out of ten of those who are unfortunate enough to catch a dose."

Already, there was one important question running through Kearns' mind: could Ebola travel through the air? Was it an airborne virus?

John Jackson answered the silent question. "We have every reason to believe that Ebola is transmittable through the air," he said. "The evidence is not yet confirmed – but it's certainly there."

"A couple of years ago," interrupted Bob Olin, "there was an outbreak down in Zaire: Ebola pretty much wiped out a whole village."

"Did they manage to contain it?" asked Kearns nervously.

"Only by burning the village to the ground," said Olin.

Kearns nodded his head and scribbled something down in

the notepad. "Gentlemen," he said, not looking up from his writing, "it seems to me that this situation calls for action of the most decisive nature."

There was a hum of agreement from the room as Kearns climbed to his feet and sought out the eyes of Tom Farr. "Out there are hundreds of people," he said gravely, pointing to the window and inwardly noting that Major Farr appeared to be the calmest person in the room. "Those hundreds of people are in daily contact with thousands more; and those thousands are the gateway to the rest of humanity – if we don't handle this properly we'll have an epidemic bigger than the Black Death on our hands."

Standing beside her husband, Judy Farr sought out his hand.

"Tom, I want you in charge of the operation," continued the General, turning towards his colleague. "I want you to lead a team up to Reston; I want it shut down; I want it made air tight, water-tight and people-tight."

Farr nodded his head to show that he understood the gravity of the situation.

"And then I want however many are left of those monkeys up there destroyed; wiped out; nuked – understand?"

Farr continued nodding.

"You can leave me to sort out the red tape on this," barked the General, who was inwardly enjoying the moment. "I'll make sure the people at Reston know that you're coming and what to expect; and I'll get on the 'phone to the White House – this situation must get to the highest level. Meanwhile, our operation has to be kept as quiet as possible – if this story breaks there'll be a national panic!"

The General's eyes turned to look at the figure of John Jackson. "I want you there, too, John," he said. "I need you to take charge of the decon facilities outside the area – if anyone gets contaminated with that bug I want them locked away!"

Tom Farr squeezed the hand of his wife and turned to face

her. He could see the fear in her eyes; he wondered if she could see his. Both partners knew what was about to happen: Reston would have to be evacuated, sealed off and placed under strict quarantine. A team of bacteriologists would be forced to handle directly contaminated monkey samples. There would be a monkey slaughter of unimaginable proportions. The only thing separating those involved from infection and the agonising death that came with it would be their orange Racal space suits. Those space suits, Farr shuddered, *those* space suits…

The sound of Tom Farr's laboured breathing filled his protective helmet as he slowly traversed the perimeter of the Reston Quarantine Unit. Farr felt faint and giddy. Sweat dripped from his forehead; he was sure that he was running a fever. His mind strayed back to the last time he had seen Dr Rosen; could the doctor have been wrong about the test results? Could he be carrying something that the standard tests did not pick up?

"Make sure that door is locked up and taped with 'no entry' signs," he said to no-one in particular, struggling to keep his voice from cracking. It was imperative that all entrances to the Unit were locked up. When the team got to work on their grisly business inside, they wanted no-one accidentally walking in on the party. It was likely that every molecule of air in that building was swimming with Ebola particles.

Farr turned to regard the thirty-or-so virus specialists that he had called into action early yesterday afternoon. They were all wearing their distinctive orange Racal pressure suits. Layers of sticky tape covered the joins between their gloves and boots. The scene reminded Farr of an episode from a sixties Sci-Fi series; the figures before him moved slowly as if undertaking a Moon walk; struggling in the bulky uniforms that made them resemble Michelin Man. Slowly, they circled the Quarantine Unit, seeking out entry points to the building. Nothing and no-one must be allowed access into this hothouse.

"You all know what is expected of you," said Farr firmly. "I want you to know that if any of you feels unable to handle this situation, there will be nothing said about it afterwards."

Farr's eyes fell on the slender form of bacteriologist Helen Grant. She was twenty four years of age. Farr had an idea that she was expecting a child. "Helen, aren't you pregnant?" he asked.

"With all due respect, Sir," came the steadfast response from behind a plastic mask, "I'd like to take a shot at this operation."

Farr shook his head impatiently. "Sorry, Helen," he said. "No way – I've seen pictures of what Ebola can do to a pregnant woman: I'm telling you – they ain't pretty."

Farr watched as the forlorn figure slowly vanished into the distance; he was still sweating; he could feel his throat tighten. This darn suit! He turned with resignation towards the main entrance of the Reston monkey house. "Everybody set?" the Major demanded.

Inside the Reston Quarantine Unit there was darkness; after the telephone call from General Kearns, the owners of the Unit had instructed Ben Leonard to clear the place out – and quick. The plug had been pulled on the building; the lights had gone; little was left of the heating system. Now all that remained were the monkeys. Because the Unit's workers had refused to go in and clean the place when they had heard the rumours about the disease, the stench of the macaques hung heavily in the air; filling the lungs of the team; making a few of them gag with nausea. With Farr leading the way, the team of virologists cautiously entered Hall H.

Shivering with the cold, the Major flicked on his flashlight and waved it around the area; immediately could be heard the panicked cries of the monkeys. Hundreds of frightened eyes stared out of the blackness at the orange-suited invaders; they could sense that something was about to happen. Farr slowly shook his head at the sight that greeted him. The monkey house was in a terrible state; beside shivering, bloody-nosed, doomed macaques lay the corpses of their brethren. The odour of decomposing bodies was intermingled with the sickly smell of monkey faeces, some of which had been spread over the walls of the building like some sad, desperate cave-painting. Farr felt the acid taste of bile rise up in his throat, but as he had last night, the Major again calmed himself down; held himself together.

"I want to warn you all right now," he said to his team as the simian cheeps of despair grew louder. "If these monkeys are infected with Ebola, one bite will be enough to kill you. Make no bones about it, these animals may be carrying enough infection to take out the whole of Washington."

One by one, Farr ran his eyes over each member of his team. "You've all read the mission plan," he said. "You all know that if we play this exactly by the rules everything will be okay. We don't want any hitches. You're working in pairs and you're *all* to follow a strict schedule, which Judy and I will now demonstrate."

The slight figure of Judy Farr moved over to join her husband; she could not see his eyes behind their plastic film. Her Racal suit was slightly too big for her; it gave her movements a comic quality. She was carrying a long metal pole that was fitted at the end with a syringe full of Ketamine, a quick-working anaesthetic. She handed it to her husband.

"If you get blood on your gloves, wipe them right away and soak them in bleach," Farr continued. "And if your suits should get a puncture – however small it is – you're to get the hell out of here."

As his words faded away, Farr cautiously edged towards the door of the nearest cage and manoeuvred the pole through its bars.

"This is the first step," he said, breathing heavily, "immobilise the monkey so that your partner can take it out."

Closely watched by his wife, Farr stared into the cage and faced its quivering occupant. The female macaque was perched on the floor near the corner. Its eyes were dull; flecks of dried green spittle were caked around its muzzle. Farr's team looked on as the Major took aim and jabbed the terrified monkey in the thigh with the knockout potion. After a few moments the powerful drug hit the animal, and it keeled over on to its side, grunting while it struggled for breath.

Satisfied that the monkey was asleep, Judy Farr opened the metal cage and stepped inside. Scanning the area for anything that might damage her protective suit, she moved over to the unconscious animal and heaved it into her arms. Silently, she carried it over to a metal table and gently laid it down. There was a slight hiss as her husband gave the creature a further injection, this time a double dose of a lethal drug named T-61.

"Aim for the heart," added Farr, sweat streaming down his forehead and into his eyes, "that's the quickest way."

Before Farr could continue there came a voice from behind him. "No!" whispered the voice, "this can't be happening!"

Startled, Farr swivelled around to face the source of the sound. His mouth gaped open in surprise when he recognised the long hair and craggy features of Ben Leonard. Farr's shocked expression was quickly replaced by a look of utter panic: Leonard, with his blue jeans and hippie regalia, did not have on a space suit! The only protection that the vet was wearing was a face mask!

"That's *all* we need – that long-haired hippie!" cried a furious Judy Farr, raising her voice into a crescendo that sent one or two monkeys flying through the air in terror.

"How the devil did you get in here?" shouted Tom Farr.

"When the General called he told me to wait for you," answered a distraught Leonard.

"Not *inside*, dummy!" screamed Judy Farr.

The Major was already on the radio to the virus containment team that waited outside. "One to come," he instructed, "a male. Get ready to douse him down!"

"Move – and quick!" ordered his wife angrily, as the veterinary doctor turned in the direction of the entrance and broke into a run.

The pale Autumn light hit Leonard like a floodlight as he reached the doors, where an airlock had been established. He felt jets of cold water rip through his clothing; he could smell bleach. Leonard closed his eyes and let the liquid soak into his body; his hair stuck to his face and his fists punched the air.

Finally, he stepped out into the frozen evening, looking like he was on fire as clouds of steam gushed out into the sky. It was then that he heard the retching noise. It was coming from somewhere close by. Leonard silently sought out the origin of the noise; it came from his left. "Ben," said a voice, "you gotta help me."

Leonard turned his head and gasped as he recognised the voice. It was one of the workers at Reston; he was also wearing no protective clothing. Leonard could not remember the name but he knew the face. A face that was currently emptying the contents of its stomach on to the black tarmac of the Unit car park. Leonard turned white as his colleague leaned towards him; there was a confused, drained look in the man's eyes. As jets of multi-coloured vomit began once more to spray from the worker's mouth, Ben Leonard slowly eased himself away.

CHAPTER EIGHT

Judy Farr turned the monkey on its side and tried to stifle a yawn. Boy, was she tired. She had lost count of how many monkeys she'd sliced apart in the three and a half hours that had elapsed since that idiot Leonard had been ordered out of the Reston Quarantine Unit. First remove the spleen; then the liver; put it in the sample box, she repeated to herself mentally, as, standing beside her, Tom Farr gave another monkey a fatal shot of T-61. The news from the outside was not good: in addition to Leonard's probable exposure to the virus, a second worker had been found wandering around the Unit; that one had been coughing his guts up. Furthermore, someone else from Reston had recently suffered a heart attack; neither man had yet tested positive for Ebola – but all the signs sure were there.

Judy's eyes moved to the ground, where a stream of bleach mixed with simian blood trickled towards a drain that had been set up in the hall; beside it stood two workers in their orange outfits. Their job was to keep swilling bleach down the drain – no-one wanted Ebola getting into the sewage system.

The smell produced by this unearthly mixture was becoming overpowering. Judy once more shot a nervous glance at her husband, who seemed to have run out of things to say as the slaughter continued. He had not spoken for the last hour and a half. Many of the team had been quiet for even longer. Most of the noise came from the simian occupants of Hall H.

Those monkeys that had not yet come down with the virus screamed their distinctive 'kra! kra!' sound; those that were too ill to react to their orange-suited executioners simply sat still and watched, taking the deadly consequences with a mere whimper. There were some animals though that were prepared to fight for their lives; hissing and biting at their captors until the anaesthetic entered their veins and they dropped to the cold floor with a soft thud.

The monkeys' tension was also beginning to affect the humans in the hall. In between fifty-minute shifts of intensified killing, they would stare blankly into the distance; breathless; tired; shocked; too overpowered by the situation to comprehend fully what they were doing.

Judy would later blame the lapse that had caused the monkey to escape on exhaustion. There was, however, a small part of her that could not help but look in the direction of Tom whenever a culprit was called for. Whatever the case, when Judy Farr opened the cage door to scoop out yet another unconscious monkey, ready to stick that needle into its heart and put an end to its existence, this one was very much awake. Either its constitution was phenomenal, or Tom had not administered the knockout jab correctly.

"Great!" Judy growled through gritted teeth as the monkey tensed its muscles and bared its pointed fangs towards her. For a frozen moment in time, their eyes met across a darkened cage. Closely related, but representatives of completely different species, the jittery human and the terrified macaque weighed up the options. What was the next move? What's the other one gonna do next? It was the monkey who answered these questions.

Springing on its haunches from the corner of the cage it had been cowering in, the male macaque flew towards Judy with blinding speed, hissing furiously; panic in its eyes. Instantly, it was upon her, and then it was gone – hurtling away at breakneck pace in the direction of Hall E, one of two other halls at Reston that was full of monkeys awaiting the death sentence.

"Judy, are you all right?" called Tom Farr, who had witnessed the incident from the corner of his eye.

His wife stood stock still, waves of nausea and shock washing over her shaking form. "Yes, I guess so," she trembled.

Farr looked into the distance; to where the monkey had escaped. He heaved a heavy sigh; getting that monkey back into its cage was not going to be easy. Farr turned his attention back to his wife and saw the imprint of the monkey's paw on her pressure suit. One-two-three-four; he could count every claw mark. Man, he could even tell if that monkey bit its nails. He also could not fail to notice that one of the claws had penetrated his wife's protective garment. The space suit had been breached; the pressure within was already beginning to wane.

Shaking, Major Farr frantically pointed towards the tear. "Get out of here, Jude," he cried. "Get out *now!*"

For the second time that afternoon, Farr reached for his radio. "One more to come," he quickly advised, "make sure there's no slip-ups."

As Farr watched his wife hurry towards the entrance to the hall, he could almost feel the adrenalin pulsing through his veins. He was also aware that his temperature had diminished; his fever seemed to be going down. Suddenly, the interior of his helmet felt less clammy.

When he'd first seen the split in his wife's suit, he'd almost lost it. Farr was ready to run; make like Dorothy's cowardly lion. Without warning, however, he felt a rush of energy flow though his body. He felt renewed; like a marathon runner getting his second wind. Once more, Farr's eyes returned to where the monkey had fled. "Any volunteers out there for a bout of Ebola-infected monkey apprehension?" he said with grim irony.

Leaving the rest of the team to carry on with the slaughter, Farr lead a group of six men into Hall E. Several of them carried syringe poles, others carried sticks with a forked 'V' at the end; with these they hoped to trap the escaped animal by its throat.

When the fleeing monkey had entered the hall, there had been howls of rage from the inmates of the cages that lined its walls. They, too, could sense that something was happening. With their superior sense of smell, the monkeys had been aware of the scent of death long before it had crept into any human nostrils. They had heard the screams of the other monkeys; they seemed resigned to the fact that their immediate future did not appear to be pleasant. With this thought ringing through their minds, the other monkeys had fought off the newcomer when it had tried to climb the bars of their cages. Already its feet and paws were dripping with blood. The other monkeys had hurled defiance and fierce blows at the subject of their anger. Its fresh, red blood now dripped from their lips.

The panic-stricken animal had no way to go; rejected by its fellow inmates, it turned its head in the direction from which it had come and desperately searched for an alternative exit. But already it could see the figures creeping slowly towards it. The ones in orange; the ones that smelt of sweat and fear – and other scents that made the macaque's eyes water. Whimpering with the voice of a two-day-old child, the monkey stood its ground and waited to fight for its survival. Meanwhile, in Hall H the killing went on.

Struggling to keep his hands from shaking, Tom Farr eased the syringe stick towards the creature. Immediately, the monkey sprang to its feet and leaped though the air, landing high up on one of the cages. As it quivered, keeping its eyes firmly on its pursuer, the inhabitant of the cage it was hanging from swiped its paws at the interloper, hissing and snorting with indignation.

"Amazing!" said one of Farr's men. "That thing jumped nearly sixteen feet."

"It'll be like trying to catch Spiderman," chipped in another.

Once more Farr pointed the stick in the direction of the

bundle of spitting fur. This time he got closer, but again the monkey produced an enormous, acrobatic leap before anchoring itself to the bars of another cage.

"Why don't we get a gun?" said the first man, who was desperate to leave the slaughterhouse and light up a cigarette.

"Because it's never been an ambition of mine to shower in Ebola blood," replied Tom Farr curtly.

This time three of them tried in vain to trap the animal. Getting the creature to stay still long enough to snag it by the throat was not proving to be easy. The chase was also beginning to agitate further the rest of the monkeys in the hall. The weary group of men wrestled with the problem for the next twenty minutes; by now some 150 monkeys had been destroyed in Hall H. The team were getting ready to repeat the exercise in the adjacent hall. Farr had an idea.

"Get some more of the sticks," he said, pointing to the 'V' tipped poles. "Get as many as you can and bring them here."

A minute or so later, six men appeared clutching the long implements. "I want you each to pick a limb; one of you take an arm, the other a leg," ordered Farr.

The Major stood up straight as he was speaking; the trapped monkey looked as if it could understand everything he was saying. "I want you to catch hold of its throat," he ordered another man. "When that's done I'm going in with this needle."

Outside Reston Quarantine Unit, Judy Farr had stripped to her underwear. In the distance she could see the lights from an armed guard that was keeping a strict vigil around the complex. Crowds of onlookers had gathered behind them to see what all the commotion was about. Beside her, in a pool of steaming bleach, lay her ruptured orange space suit. Hugging her arms to her chest, Judy scrutinised the pile of fabric, anxious to get a look at the severity of the tear. She could not help but recall the autopsies she had recently carried out on the monkeys. The poor creatures had been rampant with Ebola; their intestines had been turned into pulp and their brains to runny jelly. The images of dirty brown monkey organs were still fresh in her mind.

"Missy," a voice called out in the darkness. "Over here!"

Judy turned and clenched her aching eyes tightly shut as she was met by a hail of flashlights. This is all we need! she thought to herself in fury; newspaper reporters!

Before she could react, Judy felt warm hands upon her soaking flesh. "Get in here, Jude!" urged the familiar deep tones of John Jackson, as he pulled her into a quarantine van that was parked out of sight nearby.

Tom Farr could smell the creature's breath on his face. He had seen the look in its eyes before; he had seen the dull, glazed stare of a filovirus victim. Struggling with every fibre of its being, the animal fought to free itself from the pointed sticks that had impaled it against the wall. Tom could feel the heat of its body; he could hear the pounding of its heart. He raised the needle and plunged it into the panting animal.

Several of the other monkeys in Hall E began to hoot in terror as their trapped comrade dropped lifelessly to the concrete floor. They had seen their fate revealed to them in graphic terms; there was no room for doubt. Already some of them had turned their heads to face the rest of Farr's team, who were waiting at the entrance to Hall E ready to recommence working. "Kra! Kra! Kra!" came the chant, filling up the building and forcing the watching humans to hold their ears. "Kra! Kra! Kra!"

CHAPTER NINE

"It's done…" said Major Tom Farr, staring blankly ahead with eyes that were circled with deep black rings. "Finished… kaput… nuked. Over."

Farr was back in his military uniform, his hair still damp from the shower he had just taken. He had aged considerably in the last three days. The boyish good looks had disappeared. Sitting around him in his office were the exhausted forms of John Jackson, Bob Olin and Farr's wife, Judy. In a chair at the corner of the room sat Ben Leonard, his head cradled in his hands; his long, greasy grey hair hung limply as tears ran down his cheeks. It was 6.00 am; the team had spent over ten hours decontaminating the monkey house. All in all, over six hundred monkeys had been slaughtered and destroyed. Reston Quarantine Unit now stood empty; the silence inside telling more about what had happened there than the smell of bleach and other chemicals that lingered on.

With the sound of Leonard's sobs providing a bleak background to his words, John Jackson tried to be positive. "Well done, Tom," he said, a little too jauntily, "that was a great job you people did in there – outstanding."

"Was it?" said the Major questioningly.

"All those deaths, all that killing!" whined the voice of Ben Leonard from his seat in the corner.

"It *had* to be done," reasoned Jackson, turning towards the stricken vet. "Can't you see that there was no other way?"

"All those deaths…" repeated Leonard.

"I think we'd better get him somewhere to lie down," said Judy Farr, running her eyes over the broken Leonard before abruptly turning away, concerned that she might also burst into tears.

Without warning, the stout figure of General John Kearns strode purposefully into the subdued room carrying a newspaper under his arm. Nobody even attempted to salute him. "Ladies and gentlemen," he announced with a smile on his face. "I think that each and every one of you deserves a resounding pat on the back!"

Leonard continued his sobbing as the General sought out Tom Farr.

"Particularly you, Major Farr," he continued. "That was a first-rate job you did there – this won't go unnoticed, I can assure you of that."

A smile came to John Jackson's pockmarked face. Along with Judy Farr and Bob Olin, he had every reason to celebrate. Whilst Judy had been able to avoid any contamination from the tear in her suit, the two men had tested negative to the virus. By some miracle they had managed to survive their ill-considered decision to use that flask of Ebola as a nasal spray. All his years of experience in bacteriology told Jackson that this was wrong; the two should by now be infected with Ebola. Already their eyes should be coloured bright red and the blinding headaches should have started. The pain that they were certain to be suffering should be setting their bodies on fire, making them cry out for death. Whatever the reason for their reprieve from Death Alley, the pair of them knew one thing: theirs was an experience that could not be shared with anybody else. Jackson and Olin both had healthy pensions waiting for them when they got out of this madhouse. There was no reason to rock the boat.

"I'm glad to see that there are at least one or two smiles in the room," said the General, pulling out the newspaper and holding up its front page. "Perhaps this will make the rest of you feel a little happier."

"KILLER VIRUS UNDER CONTROL," Bob Olin quietly read out the headline that was printed in large black letters on the front cover of the *Washington Post.*

The article was accompanied by an image of a semi-naked Judy Farr. Soaked to the skin in her underwear having just discarded her Racal suit, she was standing at the entrance to Reston. The expression on her face was one of utter surprise. "My momma always said that I'd make the papers," said Judy in a weary voice.

"We tried to stop them," assured the General, "but these darn reporters are like bloodhounds – they'll follow you wherever you go."

Now it was Tom Farr who spoke: "What's the story, General?" he asked. "What about the two workers at Reston that came down with the virus?"

The General cleared his throat. "Unbelievable as it may seem," he said, "those two incidents do not appear to be related to Ebola."

"But I saw that guy chucking up his guts on the sidewalk," came the voice of Ben Leonard, as he dried his eyes with his fingers.

"Seems he only had a dose of the 'flu," replied the General. "And the other guy just had a heart-attack – it was nothing to do with the virus."

"General, that may not strictly be true," said Bob Olin, who had been listening intently to the conversation. "I've been up most of the night running tests on the samples."

"And?" said the military man.

"Put it this way," continued Olin, "I think that on this occasion we've been very, very lucky."

The room fell silent.

"The virus is *not* Ebola Zaire: it's something subtly different. It's like the Zaire strain, it's made of seven different proteins, none of which we understand. Only it's somehow different."

"Get to the point," urged Tom Farr. "We all know our basic virus theory."

"My guess is that we've just been paid a visit by a smaller

brother of Ebola Zaire. It probably hasn't got a name yet, but I'd say that, unlike the more virulent Ebola, this strain prefers to dine on monkey flesh."

"What are you saying, Bob?" said John Jackson.

"Like I said, we've been very lucky; this one just wasn't too keen on humans," replied Olin. "Admirable though our attempts at containing the virus were, if this had really been Ebola, the plague would already be sweeping through Europe by now."

"Are you *sure* of this?" asked General Kearns.

"With viruses like Ebola you can never be sure of anything," cut in Tom Farr.

"That's right," agreed Olin. "That worker who vomited up at Reston could easily have been reacting to the virus..."

The booming Southern tones of General Kearns cut him short. "This is all a little too much to take in at this time of the morning," he confessed. "I suggest we all go home and sleep on it. I'll be holding a de-briefing at fifteen hundred hours tomorrow."

Sitting next to her silent, preoccupied husband as he glided the car past crowds of early morning workers on their way to face the day, Judy Farr knew exactly what Olin had been talking about. She was acutely aware that nothing more than the shake of a dice had decided the future of her, her husband and her children. If the virus had meant business there was nothing they could have done about it. Her mind drifted through the chain of infection: a stray sneeze over breakfast would have been enough to give Richard and Karen a microscopic shower of a million Ebola particles. After a few days, the kids would have passed on the infection to hundreds of their classmates. These walking Ebola factories would all have gone home to pass it on to their families, some of whom would work at airports, shopping malls, factories. By the end of the month, the President himself could already be looking in the mirror, terrified by his red eyes and tortured by the raging headaches that made him see more than the fifty stars he was accustomed to.

Yes, Olin had been right; they had been so, so, lucky. The next time that an angry relative of the Reston virus put in an appearance on American shores, proceedings could be considerably more unpleasant.

Beside her, Major Tom Farr was also lost in his thoughts. This must not be allowed to happen again, he repeated to himself over and over. This must not be allowed to happen again. The words echoed around and around in his mind. Much work to do. Much work to do. Got to find out what makes that virus tick. We'll start tomorrow; straight after the de-brief.

Farr fished into the pocket of his uniform; his fingers found the note that been given to him by Doctor Rosen. It seemed like years ago that he had been sitting in that office. The piece of paper contained the address of the psychiatrist that the old man had recommended he go visit. Farr crinkled the paper into a ball and threw it through the open window of the car. Straight after the de-brief I'm back in that suit, he thought to himself, no time for shrinks – tomorrow I'm back in that suit… back in that space suit.

CHAPTER TEN

David Crosby singin' Tambourine Man, boy you couldn't beat it, thought Ben Leonard as he stepped into Hall H of the Reston Quarantine Unit with a spring in his step and a Byrds compilation in his Walkman. It almost made you feel good to be alive.

In the six months or so since the incident with the filovirus, the monkey house had gradually regained a semblance of normality. Once more the high-pitched cries of the monkeys reverberated around the hall. The acrid smell of bleach had slowly been replaced by a scent which Leonard felt more comfortable with: Eau de Macaque; the smell that his monkeys made as they went about their daily business. The petty squabbles and disputes; the playful acrobatics.

It had not been easy for Leonard to return to his job. Even though he had lost count of the number of simian autopsies that he had performed over the years, Leonard could not forget the look in those monkeys' eyes that awful night. The terrified, whimpering fear on all of their faces as they waited in a queue labelled 'death'. For a while, Leonard had considered a change of career; somewhere safer and quieter – but in the end he had just found himself missing the animals too much.

Leonard had been present at the Unit to supervise the arrival of the first shipment of monkeys to be brought to Reston after the virus outbreak. He had watched as teams of men from the Institute had carefully checked to see that all traces of the virus had been eliminated. He had even run his own tests when the army men had gone home. Leonard was surprised how easy it had been to fall back in the old routine. Straight away there were animals to be cleaned;

sick monkeys to be treated – a million and one things to do.

He had never quite forgiven the people at USAMRIID for what they had done to his monkeys; particularly that smug-faced Major and his ill-mannered witch of a wife. Leonard told himself that there *could* have been another way. There was no reason to murder all those animals. There might have been survivors. But then Leonard would remember how he himself had felt after his own exposure to the virus; then he would have slaughtered a thousand monkeys if it could have somehow rid him of the disease. This was an attitude that, unsurprisingly, had been swiftly amended when Leonard later tested negative for Ebola Zaire.

It had been three months since the Institute had last paid him a visit. There had, of course, been the inevitable post mortems on the events of last autumn. Leonard could not forget the drudgery of sitting through endless interminable meetings; being examined and cross-examined by the men in suits. Even then he knew that it was all pointless. The authorities responded as if they had been vindicated when it had been discovered that the Ebola strain which hit Reston was harmless to humans. How could they have done anything wrong when there had never been any danger to anybody during the operation? The Institute maintained that they had merely reacted with due care and attention to an outbreak of a foreign strain of simian disease. Leonard would have put money on the fact that the Reston report probably lay in a file at the back of some dusty cabinet. USAMRIID no longer even considered his monkey house a risk. Leonard played with his wooden beads as the thoughts raced around his mind.

There was a part of him that inwardly believed the army people had probably enjoyed their experience; it had given them the chance to get out of the office and flex their military muscles. But at least Leonard was here to make sure that they never again returned with their syringe sticks and lethal drugs. The veterinary doctor had worked hard to make his monkey house the cleanest and most hygienic in the land. Health checks on the macaques had been tripled; the straw in their cages changed twice a day.

In the days before the outbreak, Leonard would probably have already been home by now. He would have been settling down in front of the TV with a cold beer. As it was, it was 7.00 pm and he was still working. Leonard didn't really mind though; these days he found it hard to sleep if he hadn't taken a last look at the monkeys before he left Hall H.

Although the last batch of monkeys had only arrived three days ago, Leonard had already found his favourite. Slightly smaller and skinnier than any of the others, it possessed a spiteful and vindictive temper. It would, however, allow Leonard close if he brought food with him. He had named it 'Judy'.

"C'mon Jude," Leonard called in a playful voice, "come to daddy."

As usual, the vet's Chosen One was playing hard to get. The macaque sat on the floor of its cage, stubbornly refusing to respond to the tempting delights of the monkey biscuit that Leonard was waving at it. "Quit messing around!" he smiled.

Leonard always marvelled at the individual personalities that his monkeys possessed. You could definitely pick up human characteristics in the majority of them.

There was the street-mugger, with its low hairline and quick, hungry eyes; and there was the shy one, too blushing and bashful to come near a human; then there were the ones like Judy: haughty; aristocratic; a law unto themselves.

"I guess you're not hungry," he called to the female macaque, pretending to nibble the end of the biscuit himself. "Well if you don't want it, I'm feelin' kinda hungry myself."

As he peered with affection down into the cage, a frown slowly appeared on Leonard's face. "What's wrong, Jude?"

he muttered with concern.

Feeling himself go numb, Leonard gazed deeply into the monkey's eyes. They were dull and lifeless; it was like there was no-one home. He had seen those eyes somewhere before. Leonard gave a gasp and slowly opened his mouth as he noticed the trickle of blood running from the creature's heaving nostrils.

Glossary

AMPLIFICATION
This term is used to describe what happens when a virus enters a host and begins to replicate itself. In effect, the host's cells are transformed into virus cells.

CHEMTURION SPACE SUIT
A pressurised, heavy-duty biological space suit worn when working with a Biosafety Level 4 virus such as Ebola or Marburg.

DECON
A military term, meaning decontaminate.

EBOLA
Pronounced 'ee-boh-la', an extremely lethal virus from the tropics that has three known strains: Ebola Zaire; Ebola Sudan; and Ebola Reston, which is named after the outbreak at the Reston monkey house.

ELECTRON MICROSCOPE
A large and extremely powerful microscope which operates by firing a beam of electrons to magnify the image of a very small object such as a virus cell. It is then displayed on a screen, where it can be photographed.

ENVIROCHEM
A green-coloured disinfectant used to kill viruses in airlock chemical showers.

FILOVIRUS
Also known as thread viruses, a family of viruses that comprise Ebola and Marburg only. Under the microscope the virus resembles a mass of crawling worms.

GREY AREA; GREY ZONE
The room between a hot zone and the normal world.

HIV
Human immunodeficiency virus – the cause of AIDS. This disease is a Level 2 agent, and is, therefore, much harder to contract than Ebola or Marburg. Unlike filoviruses, HIV can only be passed on to another human being through blood or body fluids.

HOST
An organism – such as a human being or a monkey – that becomes infected by a virus or disease.

HOT
In military jargon, lethally infective in biological terms.

HOT AGENT
An extremely lethal disease such as Ebola or Marburg that can be potentially carried through the air.

HOT SUITE
A collection of Biosafety Level 4 laboratories.

HOT ZONE
An area that contains lethally infective diseases such as Marburg or Ebola.

MARBURG VIRUS
A disease that is very closely related to Ebola – it was originally named Stretched Rabies.

NUKE
A word used in biology to describe an attempt to render an area sterile.

RACAL SUIT
A positive-pressure space suit used to prevent humans from coming into contact with a lethal disease. Possessing a battery-powered air supply, it is used in field work. Because of their distinctive colour, they are sometimes called orange suits.

REPLICATION
This occurs when a virus has infected a host and begins to copy itself and grow.

SENTINEL ANIMAL
An animal such as a monkey used by biologists to detect the presence of a lethal disease. If an area is infected, the creature will succumb to the disease; in doing so it prevents humans from risking their lives.

SHF
Simian haemorrhagic fever. A virus that is lethal to monkeys but harmless to human beings.

SLAMMER
The Biosafety Level 4 containment hospital at USAMRIID.

STERILISATION
The total destruction of all living beings, including animals and microscopic bacteria, within a pre-defined area. This is difficult to achieve and almost impossible to verify.

THIRD SPACING
Enormous haemorrhagic bleeding beneath the skin.

USAMRIID
United States Army Medical Research Institute of Infectious Diseases, at Fort Detrick, in Frederick, Maryland. It is also known as the Institute.

VIRUS
A microscopic disease-carrying agent consisting of a shell made from proteins and membranes and a core containing DNA or RNA. A virus requires a living agent in order to replicate.

Biographies

This story contains fictional characters investigating a true-life mystery. Before you look at the facts and make up your own mind, here is a brief biography of the characters:

MAJOR THOMAS FARR
(FICTIONAL)

An expert in diseases, forty-two-year-old Farr is the man in charge of USAMRIID. He is ideally placed for such a role, having undertaken an extensive tour of Africa on the lookout for exotic diseases.

DOCTOR JUDY FARR
(FICTIONAL)

The wife of Major Farr, Judy is an expert in the isolation and treatment of rare viruses. At thirty two years of age, she is also employed by USAMRIID, and is the most experienced member of the Institute when dealing with monkeys.

GENERAL JOHN D. KEARNS
(FICTIONAL)

General Kearns is the head of USAMRIID, but prefers to leave the day-to-day running of the Institute to his protégé, Thomas Farr. His experience with foreign diseases is limited.

BENJAMIN LEONARD
(FICTIONAL)
Notorious for his unconventional approach to medicine, the doctor of veterinary medicine works at the Reston Quarantine Unit. In charge of Hall H, one of three large halls each containing up to 450 hundred monkeys, Leonard often lets his feelings get in the way of the job he is employed to do.

JOHN JACKSON
(FICTIONAL)
Also employed by USAMRIID, Doctor John Jackson works in the viral laboratories at the Institute, where he is a key figure in the research of rare diseases. Jackson's face and body are heavily scarred with smallpox, which he contracted on a field trip to South East Asia.

ROBERT OLIN
(FICTIONAL)
John Jackson's closest friend at USAMRIID, Olin also works in the laboratories, assisting his colleague with viral research.

CLASSIFIED FILES

How was it possible for a diseased consignment of monkeys to arrive unnoticed at a quarantine unit barely three miles from the White House? Who was responsible for this potentially lethal mistake? Could this frightening event happen again? Here are the answers to some of these questions.

 How did a colony of infected monkeys come to arrive at Reston Quarantine Unit?

On Wednesday 14 October 1989 Hazelton Research Products took charge of a shipment of monkeys imported from the Philippines. The monkeys came from Ferlite Farms, a monkey export facility close to the capital, Manila. Housed in wooden crates, the animals entered New York City via Amsterdam. They eventually arrived at JFK airport and were transferred by truck to the Reston monkey house, where they were placed under the care of colony manager Bill Volt.

Two of the monkeys were already dead on arrival at Reston. Although Volt realised that the deaths were not an unusual occurrence (monkeys would often find the trauma of the journey too much for them), he became extremely concerned by the beginning of November, when more of the monkeys began to die. It was becoming clear that they had fallen victim to an unknown virus of which Volt had no previous experience. On 1 November, Volt called up simian disease expert Dan Dalgard, to take a look at the creatures for himself.

Dalgard was immediately concerned by what he saw and proposed that he perform an autopsy on one of the dead animals. When he cut the carcass open. Dalgard was surprised to discover that the animal's innards had been completely destroyed by the strange ailment; he had a hunch that they might be dealing with simian fever (SHF). The vet failed to notice that the obliterated state of the monkey's internal organs was a classic symptom of a Level 4 filovirus such as Marburg. Nevertheless, Dalgard was sufficiently worried to make a call to USAMRIID, where he spoke to a civilian virologist named Peter Jahrling.

Jahrling requested that Dalgard send some samples over to the Institute, which was barely a half-hour drive away from Reston monkey house. These arrived by courier the following morning, badly wrapped in metal foil that was dripping with monkey blood. Volt, of course, had no way of knowing that the samples contained a potentially lethal strain of Ebola. Had he been aware, there is no doubt Jahrling would have ensured that the deadly cargo was transported to USAMRIID in a more suitable and safer manner.

Jahrling carried the monkey samples into a Level 3 laboratory and set about making a culture. This procedure involved growing cell samples in a test tube warmed to body temperature. Jahrling hoped that any disease held in the sample would replicate, allowing him to get a better look at the mystery agent under the microscope at a later date.

Whilst Jahrling had been working, Dan Dalgard had also been busy back at Reston. As the monkeys continued to succumb to the unknown predator, Dalgard opened up eight of the carcasses in a vain attempt to understand what was killing them. Becoming increasingly confused by the whole sequence of events, Dalgard placed the remains in a chest freezer at the end of Hall H.

On Friday 17 November, Thomas Geisbert, an electron microscope operator employed by USAMRIID, decided to take a look at the flasks of monkey cells that, four days earlier, had been placed in the Level 3 laboratory by his colleague, Peter Jahrling. Before putting them under the enormous tower of the electron microscope, Geisbert elected to examine them first under a light microscope. Unlike its giant younger brother, a light microscope still uses lenses to focus light on the subject. The magnification is nowhere near as powerful as the electron microscope but Geisbert was confident that he could still get a pretty good look at the sample. When he placed his eye to the lens, Geisbert immediately knew that he was looking at something completely outside the bounds of his experience. The contents of the flask had been devastated by whatever had killed them. The milky fluid contained cells whose very structure had been ripped apart by a powerful and deadly killer. And amongst the residue of dead and dying cellular matter, Geisbert could see black flecks of material; it was almost as if someone had shaken pepper over the toxic mixture. The twenty-seven-year-old Geisbert decided to fetch his boss Peter Jahrling.

Jahrling's first reaction on seeing the samples was that they had been in some way contaminated; that a wild strain of bacteria had invaded the cell culture. This was not an unusual occurrence – in such cases the samples were simply thrown away and a new culture begun. To confirm his thoughts, Jahrling unscrewed the lid from the flask and held it to his nose. One of the first signs that a culture has gone bad is when it starts to smell. A cell culture that has gone bad can smell like the worst rotting eggs. Like Thomas Geisbert, Jahrling had been taught this at college and thought nothing of using his sense of smell to test the mixture. He was very surprised when he could smell nothing; although the sample looked as if it has been contaminated, no odour at all emanated from the residue. Jahrling handed the flask to his colleague, who also took a sniff and agreed that there was no apparent odour. The contents of the flask puzzled both men. Geisbert and Jahrling decided that the next step would be to place the sample under the electron microscope and take a closer look at whatever was going on in that mysterious flask.

It was ten days later before the sample found its way under the electron microscope. The enigma of the virus from Reston was still low on Thomas Geisbert's list of priorities; it was one of many problems to be dealt with on his busy work schedule. Certainly, a contaminated cell sample was not enough to drag Geisbert away from the pre-Thanksgiving Day celebrations that marked the end of November.

What Geisbert saw under the electron microscope was enough to set his pulse racing. Under powerful magnification the extent of the damage to the cell samples could clearly be seen. The cells were blown apart and appeared to be crawling with worms. It was the worms that troubled Geisbert the most. He knew that the only type of virus that resembled worms was a filovirus – possibly Marburg. A killer for which there is no known cure. Geisbert had seen pictures of the Marburg virus but had never seen it at first hand. Although by no means an expert on the effects of filoviruses, Geisbert was aware that USAMRIID would have a major problem on its hands if his suspicions were confirmed. Once again, Geisbert went to see Peter Jahrling and shared his concerns.

Jahrling did not have to look at Geisbert's photographs of the virus for long to realise that he could be approaching the biggest crisis of his career. If the monkey house in Reston was infected with Marburg it could be only a matter of days before the disease hit the streets of Washington DC. Furthermore, both he and Geisbert had sniffed at the flask containing the monkey sample. They could already be incubating the disease as he spoke. Jahrling called in his boss, Colonel C. J. Peters.

The forthright Peters was initially sceptical when he was shown the photographs of the samples; he, too, immediately assumed that the flask had simply been contaminated with bacteria. However, he did not want to take any chances; as chief of the disease assessment division at USAMRIID, Peters could not risk the consequences of not reacting to a situation like this – even if he was not yet convinced that a filovirus was on the loose. Peters instructed his two colleagues to conduct more tests while he got on the telephone to Reston Quarantine Unit and requested that he be allowed to pick up more specimens.

Later that evening whilst Peters was busy at Reston, the diligent Jahrling and Geisbert managed to identify the virus. It was a new strain of Ebola; almost identical in appearance to Ebola Zaire, but subtly different. By the time the outbreak had run its course, the new strain would become known as Ebola Reston.

Peters acted quickly when he heard the news; the army man mobilised a decon unit and resolved to enter the monkey house and destroy all the animals that it housed. The perimeter of Reston Quarantine Unit was surrounded by armed guards to prevent any unwanted visitors wandering into the area. On Thursday 30 November, a team of bacteriologists wearing Racal orange space suits entered the building. During the course of the day some 65 animals were destroyed in Hall H of the Unit. By the following Tuesday evening a further 450 monkeys had been killed.

The team inside Reston had been shocked to see the extent of the infection. Nearly all the monkeys carried the disease. And yet, surprisingly, no human had yet come down with the illness. Jahrling and Geisbert had both tested negative for Ebola, as had two Reston workers, who had been suspected of having the disease. Somehow a crisis had been averted.

The Reston Quarantine Unit was thoroughly decontaminated using a mixture of bleach and EnviroChem and pronounced clean. It was announced that the virus was a new strain of Ebola; one that was fatal to monkeys but did not seem to affect humans. It appeared that Mother Nature had given humans a warning. The staff at USAMRIID were only too aware that they had been very lucky – had the disease possessed a penchant for human flesh the result could have been very different.

The Institute's relief, however, was short-lived. A month later the virus reappeared at Reston. This time, since there had been no loss to human life, it was decided to let the disease run its course. It did, so with devastating efficiency; drifting through the air to infect the new stocks of monkeys with deadly Ebola Reston until no animal was alive. This was Ebola's last recorded visit to the United States – who knows when it will return again?

WHAT IF RESTON *HAD* BEEN HARMFUL TO HUMANS?

If it had been Ebola Zaire that had hit Reston in 1989 it is unlikely that you would be here to read this book.

The first westerners in the chain of infection would probably have been the staff that took receipt of the monkey shipment at JFK airport. At the same time that Dan Dalgard had begun to notice the strange disease that was afflicting his animals, the airport workers would already be on their way around the globe, landing at other airports and spreading the invisible killer.

Dalgard would most likely have been the first person in Reston to come down with Ebola. He would have been quickly joined on the sick list by Peter Jahrling and Thomas Geisbert, whose coughs and sneezes would have soon infected everyone they came into contact with at USAMRIID. Within forty-eight hours the disease would have spread from coast to coast. In under two weeks, nine out of ten citizens in America would be dead, with the rest of the world following closely behind this frightening statistic.

You would most probably have caught it from your friends at school.

What is Ebola and how does it spread?

Ebola is a Level 4 filovirus (a corruption of the Latin for 'thread') that was first identified in the Ebola region of Zaire in 1976. Like its close relative, Marburg, Ebola can be transmitted in many ways: through the air via the sneezes of its agonised hosts, or through blood and body fluids. There is no known cure for the disease, which has an incubation period of 10 to 13 days and a mortality rate of 90 per cent.

Where does Ebola come from?

Nobody can be completely sure where diseases such as Ebola and Marburg originate. Some experts believe that the virus is millions of years old. They speculate that the deadly microscopic cells lay dormant in Africa until people began destroying the country's vast forests and jungles. It was only then that they came into contact with this most patient of killers.

There have been many expeditions into Africa to discover the origin of Ebola. There are some who are convinced that the source of the virus lies within a small cave at the base of Mount Elgon, overlooking Lake Victoria. Kitum Cave is in many ways unusual; not least for the fact that it is not a naturally occurring geological phenomenon. Its enormous, bat-infested interior has been created by the tusks of elephants. Over millions of years, massive herds of these great beasts that have grazed in the area have been attracted to Kitum Cave because of its salt deposits. Whilst digging out the mineral that is necessary to their survival, they have carved out the colossal opening and, perhaps, set free a killer.

Inside Kitum Cave, where the wearing of a protective space suit is compulsory, is an underground stream that flows with cool, clear water. It is from here that the Ebola virus is said to originate. Visitors to the site are strongly advised to bring their own drinking water.

Where was the first outbreak of Ebola?

The first case of Ebola occurred in 1976 in the town of Zazra, in southern Sudan. The first victims suffered from fevers and aching joints; these symptoms were quickly followed by kidney failure, bleeding and death. The disease spread to a nearby hospital, infecting staff and patients. More than half of its 300 victims died.

Ebola made its second appearance two months later in the Ebola River region of Zaire, and on this occasion almost provoked a global emergency. It occurred at a mission

hospital and with frightening ferocity killed
14 out of 17 staff workers. One nurse, on
the brink of death, was transported from the
area to the country's capital city, Kinshasa.
Fearing a pandemic, the country's authorities
had the Zairean army cordon off the area
whilst an international scientific team was
hurriedly dispatched to Kinshasa.

What are the symptoms of Ebola?

The Ebola virus is a perfectly designed human parasite. It attacks the body tissue and internal organs, turning them into a mushy slime of Ebola cells. In effect, Ebola transforms the host into itself. Ebola is comprised of seven unidentified proteins; when combined these create the perfect killing machine. Once it has found a host, the virus's initial attacks go unnoticed. Before any external symptoms are apparent, the virus has already been working to disable the body's systems by destroying blood cells and turning them into more virus. Within a week, all of the body's internal organs are beginning to die, themselves becoming millions of infectious Ebola cells.

The first sign that a victim is carrying Ebola comes with a painful migraine that no amount of painkillers can relieve. This is usually followed by a reddening of the eyes which can give the terrified sufferer the appearance of a blood-starved zombie. Then comes the haemorrhagic rash, when strips of skin split open and blood pours from the lips. By this time the victim does not have long to live. Blood begins to pour from every orifice, whilst the surface of the tongue grows red until it peels off. This sloughing of the tongue is said to be incredibly painful, but the worst is yet to come. As death approaches, the sufferer may go blind and cry tears of blood. By now the blood is refusing to coagulate and flows like a river; any pain-killing injections that are administered will only serve to heighten the torment. After ten days of this torture, the body's internal organs cease to function; swollen out of all recognition, they begin to putrefy and turn into crystal-like blocks. These blocks are full of Ebola spores that will soon 'burst', showering the immediate vicinity with virus. Finally, the patient will go into epileptic convulsions and die, spurting geysers of blood into the surroundings. It is thought that this way of death is a deliberate act by the virus; a means, perhaps, of ensuring its survival by quickly locating new hosts.

After death, the body of the victim undergoes a rapid deterioration. All internal organs and body tissue begin to dissolve away. As the body liquefies, a microscopic universe of Ebola cells begin the search for a fresh victim.

THE BLACK DEATH

Along with AIDS, filoviruses such as Ebola and Marburg represent a terrible threat to the survival of humanity. However, these diseases are relative newcomers compared with the bubonic plague, a disease that decimated Europe in the 14th-century and returned to wreak havoc on London society two hundred years later. The story of what happened all those centuries ago during the Black Death serves as a succinct reminder of what a killer virus can do when it is out of control.

How did the Black Death reach Europe?

The Black Death first reached Europe from China in the summer of 1347. In October of that year, a Genoese fleet landed at Sicily, carrying rats on board that had the sickness. By winter the plague was in Italy, and by January 1348, it had reached Marseilles. In September 1348, the Black Death reached the shores of England.

What is the Black Death?

Bubonic plague is the medical term for the Black Death. It is caused by a bacillus – an organism that is usually carried by rodents. The disease is passed on to humans via the fleas that infest these small animals. Once it has jumped on to a human, the flea regurgitates the blood from the rat into the new host. Symptoms include high fevers, aching limbs and vomiting of blood. Most noticeable is a swelling of the lymph nodes; these glands are situated in the neck, armpits and groin. The swellings protrude and continue to expand until they eventually burst and death follows. The blackish colouring of the swellings earned the disease its name. Victims usually die only four days after exhibiting feverish symptoms similar to 'flu.

What happened when the disease hit Europe in the 14-century?

Although bubonic plague still exists today in some parts of the world, it is not always fatal. Modern medicine possesses drugs which can cure the illness if administered in time. In the 1340s, however, things were very different. The science of medicine was still in its infancy; doctors could only begin to guess at the cause of the plague. They had no choice but to sit and watch the dead bodies pile up.

When the disease entered a new town or city, its impact on the populace was immediate. Within days, there was a new scent in the air: the odour of decaying bodies. Here a contemporary account describes what happened when the disease entered Messina in Sicily:

At the beginning of October, in the year of the incarnation of the Son of God 1347, twelve Genoese galleys entered the harbour of Messina. In their bones they bore so virulent a disease that anyone who only spoke to them was seized by a mortal illness and in no manner could evade death. The infection spread to everyone who had any contact with the diseased. Those infected felt themselves penetrated by a pain throughout their whole bodies. Then there developed on the thighs or upper arms a boil about the size of a lentil which the people called 'burn boil'. This infected the whole body, and penetrated it so that the patient violently vomited blood. This continued without intermission for three days, there being no means of healing it, and then the patient expired.

When faced with the mysterious illness that had no cure, the people of Messina panicked. Some townsfolk fled the area – and in doing so spread the infection to other towns and cities. Others blamed witchcraft for the catastrophe that had befallen them. Many simply lay in their beds and waited to die. The Church authorities of the day could do nothing to prevent the disease from rampaging its way across the countryside.

Contrary to popular belief, the public officials of the time did not blame the calamity on the wrath of God. They realised that it was a disease which was wiping out the population, and took whatever steps they could to halt its progress. Their knowledge of bubonic plague was, however, limited in the extreme. They had no idea how it was being transmitted.

With mass poverty and overcrowded, unsanitary conditions, cities were the hardest hit by the Black Death. Many tried in vain to control the spread of the virus. In Milan, for example, city officials immediately walled up houses found to have the plague, locking the healthy in with the sick and causing greater loss of life.

How did they try to stop the spread of the plague?

Because the smell from the dead and dying was so awful, many people believed that the disease was transmitted through the air. The living doused themselves in scents to ward off the illness. All kinds of incense were burned to no avail; whilst handkerchiefs were dipped in aromatic oils to cover the face when going out. Also used were talismans, charms and spells that could be purchased from the local wise woman or from the apothecary.

In 1348 the Pope dispatched a team to

Paris in order to study the effects of the plague. Its subsequent report concluded that the disaster had been caused by a particularly unfortunate conjunction of Saturn, Jupiter and Mars in the sign of Aquarius that had occurred in 1345. This conjunction, it decreed, produced hot, moist conditions, which in turn caused the Earth to exhale poisonous vapours.

The report went on to recommend steps to keep safe from the disease:

No poultry should be eaten, no waterfowl, no pig, no old beef, altogether no fat meat ...It is injurious to sleep during the daytime ...Fish should not be eaten, too much exercise may be injurious ...Nothing should be cooked in rainwater. Olive oil with food is deadly ...Bathing is dangerous.

The town officials had no way of knowing that the only real way of avoiding the disease was by isolation: staying away from sufferers so that fleas were unable to reach a new host.

 How many people succumbed to the Black Death?

• Between 45% and 75% of the population of Florence died in a single year; a third of which died in the first six months.

• In Venice, 60% died over the course of 18

months. At the height of the outbreak 500 to 600 people died each day.

• Even when the worst of the plague was over, smaller outbreaks continued for centuries afterwards. The people of the Middle Ages lived in constant fear of the plague's return; and the disease did not disappear until the 1600s.

• Overall between one third and one half of the population of Europe died during the Black Death.

How did the plague affect Britain?

The most recent outbreak of the Black Death in Europe occurred in England in 1665. The Great Plague of London decimated the capital's population and was only halted when the Great Fire of that year razed the city to the ground. Had the blaze that began in Pudding Lane not destroyed London's flourishing rat community it is likely that the loss of life would have been considerably higher.

THE MAN WHO SURVIVED A FILOVIRUS

On the morning of 8 January 1980 Charles Monet woke up with a headache; a dull throbbing pain behind his temples that had begun the night before. Originally from France, Monet had moved to Africa a year earlier and was working at a local sugar factory in a small town named Nzoia. Some days before, Monet had taken a sightseeing tour of Mount Elgin, which was located a few miles away from the town. He was known among his workmates as a loner, so no-one took any notice when Monet did not turn up for work that day, nor was there any concern when he failed to show up for the rest of the week.

It was Monet's housekeeper who discovered the whereabouts of the Frenchman. She found him lying in bed, running a high fever, and endeavoured to take care of him. Three days after he had first developed the headache, Monet felt nauseous and began vomiting. At the same time, his appearance seemed to change; his eyelids drooped and his skin took on a cold, lifeless quality. When Monet's workmates finally paid their errant colleague a visit they were appalled by his condition and immediately drove him to a private hospital in the nearby city of Kisumu. After the antibiotics that the doctors prescribed had had no effect on their patient, it was decided that Monet should travel by airplane to Nairobi Hospital, which was bigger and had better facilities than their own. Because Monet could still walk, he was obliged to take a taxi to the airport and board the plane alone.

Once aboard the craft, Monet's condition worsened considerably. During the flight, he began to vomit blood. Fellow passengers aboard the craft looked at each other nervously as the Frenchman hunched over his seat and continued to be sick for the rest of the flight. His appearance was shocking; his eyes had sunk into their sockets and his skin was stretched over his skull like a death mask. Incredibly, the terribly sick Monet managed to stumble out of the plane when it eventually landed and hail a taxi. As the car traversed the streets of Nairobi, the driver kept a fearful eye on his passenger, who was once again vomiting deep red blood.

Charles Monet entered the casualty department of Nairobi Hospital and managed to mumble a few words before being told to take a seat. As soon as he had sat down Monet began to die. As the room began to spin around him, Monet bent over and brought up more blood; blood that poured on to the floor and began to make its way into the corridor.

While the other patients sitting nearby edged nervously away from the violently convulsing Frenchman, nurses and aides rushed to the scene and placed Monet on to a trolley. Quickly, he was wheeled into the Intensive Care unit of the hospital and a young doctor named Shem Musoke was summoned to help. Dr Musoke arrived to find Charles Monet bleeding heavily and fighting for his breath. Then Monet stopped breathing.

The young doctor immediately ordered a laryngoscope – a tube that is used to open a patient's airway. Musoke put his fingers into the dying Frenchman's mouth and cleared away a mixture of black vomit and bile that was blocking the airway. Then he eased open Monet's lips and inserted the laryngoscope into the heaving man's mouth. At that moment, Monet began to vomit again; a shower of red and black liquid hit Dr Musoke full in the face, running into his mouth and eyes. As Dr Musoke spat out the vile mixture his patient began to breathe once more.

Musoke and his staff were shocked to see the amount of bleeding; crimson blood seemed to be coming from every part of the man's body. In vain, Musoke attempted a blood transfusion but this only worsened matters; each new prick from the syringe would create a fresh fountain of unstaunchable blood.

Eventually the newcomer fell into a coma. Dr Musoke stayed with him until Charles Monet passed away in the early hours of the next morning.

Nine days after the patient was admitted to Nairobi Hospital Shem Musoke himself began to feel a headache. The pain soon spread to his joints and back, but this paled into insignificance when the doctor caught a sight of himself in the mirror. Musoke was horrified to see that his eyes had turned bright red. At first Musoke wondered if he had somehow contracted a dose of malaria. After taking some malaria pills, Musoke even had one of the nurses give him a jab for the disease. He had been quite unprepared for the pain that hit him during the injection. As he began to feel more and more sick, Musoke presented himself to a colleague at the hospital, Dr Bagshawe.

Having never witnessed such severe symptoms before, the doctor incorrectly diagnosed that Musoke was suffering from a gall bladder attack or kidney infection. She immediately placed him into investigative surgery. When Musoke was opened up Dr Bagshawe was puzzled to see that Musoke's liver was swollen out of all recognition. Furthermore, there was no way that they could stop him from bleeding. It was almost as if he had become a haemophiliac. Every artery seemed to pump blood. One of Musoke's colleagues remembered being 'up to the elbows in blood'.

After the operation, Musoke's condition worsened. His kidneys began to give out; the doctor seemed to be dying. Running out of ideas, Dr Bagshawe dispatched samples of Monet's blood to the National Institute of Virology in Sandringham, South Africa, and to the Center for Disease Control at Atlanta, Georgia, USA.

Forty-eight hours later, an American doctor named David Silverstein, who was practising in Nairobi, received a phone call at his home in the early hours of the morning. The call was from an American researcher stationed in Kenya, who reported that the South Africans had discovered something strange in the blood sample of Shem Musoke. They informed him that the blood sample was infected with the Marburg virus. Unable to sleep, the American located a reference work on Marburg. There he learned that Marburg is a Level 4 filovirus with a more than fifty per cent mortality rate. Once he had read of the disease's effect on the human body, Silverstein persuaded the Nairobi authorities to shut down the hospital.

In all some sixty-seven people were held in

quarantine. Medical staff who had operated on Musoke were forced to wait and see if they, too, had contracted the virus. Incredibly, there were no further Marburg victims. Even more amazingly, after 10 days of drifting in and out of a coma, Dr Musoke began to show signs of improvement. Eventually, his fever subsided and he began to return to normality. He could remember nothing of his brush with a deadly killer. Within months Musoke was back at work. He had been very lucky. Samples of the doctor's blood were dispatched to research facilities around the world, where they are kept in Level 4 containment laboratories. Today the species of Marburg virus that attacked the African doctor and killed Charles Monet is known as the Musoke strain.

CLASSIFIED

Reader, your brief is to be on the alert for the following spine-tingling books.

CLASSIFIED SERIES:

☐ The Internet Incident   Ian Probert   £2.99

☐ Encounter on the Moon   Robin Moore £2.99

☐ Discovery at Roswell   Terry Deary £2.99

☐ The Philadelphia Experiment Terry Deary £2.99

☐ The Nuclear Winter Man   Terry Deary £2.99

☐ Break Out!   Terry Deary £2.99

☐ Area 51   Robin Moore £2.99

☐ Virus Outbreak   Ian Probert   £2.99

Stay tuned for further titles. Over and out.